CLARITY

CLARITY

By Arlene Goldbard

iUniverse, Inc.
New York Lincoln Shanghai

Clarity

iUniverse, Inc.
an imprint of iUniverse, Inc.

For information address:
iUniverse
2021 Pine Lake Road, Suite 100
Lincoln, NE 68512
www.iuniverse.com

Author Photo credit: Averie Cohen © 2004.

ISBN: 0-595-31531-3

Printed in the United States of America

Blessings to my friends who so generously read, commented on, and supported me in creating this book. What is good in it owes much to their help, while any mistakes are my own.
Any resemblance to actual persons is entirely in aid of satire, which happily has not yet been outlawed.

CHAPTER 1

Once upon a time, neither very long ago nor all that far away, there lived a woman called Dina Meyer. She made her home in the capital of a place slightly more imaginary than real, that large and various state known as California. Her employer was the sovereign of that land, its elected governor, and she toiled at his pleasure at one of the intricate and challenging tasks of turn-of-the-century public life. It was Dina's job to navigate the mazes and tunnels through which information must pass to reach the citizenry in its intended form. Dina was a press secretary, though she hated to say so.

In fact, she had lately come to hate so many things she was called upon to say and do that she often found it tough to rouse herself from sleep to face them. It was in her nature to defeat difficulties through acts of will. Consequently, she addressed her reluctance to arise in the morning by forcing herself to awaken earlier than necessary, stationing a particularly loud and obnoxious alarm clock on a table some distance from her bed. Throughout the winter, this virtuously self-punishing strategy had a bracing if paradoxical effect: it pried Dina out of bed and into contact with the world outside; it also gave her one more thing (the alarm clock) and one more person (herself, for setting it) to hate.

But as the season changed, things began to look different. Rising early gave Dina time alone to enjoy the sights and scents of spring in the smoothness of first light, before the daily epidemic of urgencies and imperatives disfigured the world. Thus, by mid-April she had two fewer things to hate and many more in which to delight.

On this particular morning, Dina stepped out of the house into air that was cool and fragrant against her skin, like petals in the breeze. Tender green leaflets preened on their delicate branches, clamoring for attention. Peering down the street, Dina awarded herself yet another early-riser's gold star: she was reliably first on her block to fetch the morning paper. A row of bright plastic bags dotted the chain of driveways, swimming-pool blue for the local paper, the *Sacramento Bee*, rain-slicker yellow for the *San Francisco Chronicle*. Dina read the *New York Times* online at work, figuring two daily papers was enough of a burden to put on the recycling system.

Alice the cat slithered along Dina's right leg, depositing a clump of gray fur on the fleece of her slipper. Three doors down, a man in plaid pajama bottoms shuffled to the sidewalk, stooping to pick up the day's news. Dina saluted her neighbor, silently bestowing the silver star. Smiling and waving his paper, he pressed one hand to the small of his back, coaxing his spine to face the day.

Once around the liquidambar tree and Alice sidled back to mark the left slipper. Most days, Dina darted out the front door for a surgical strike on the paper, snatching it up and returning to the house without stopping, swift as a Pony Express rider. Something slightly indecent about the way her mother had done her outside chores in a housecoat—setting the sprinklers, leaving the mail for the postman—usually kept Dina from lingering on the front walk of a morning. Not that she resembled Charlotte in this way: instead of pink nylon and graying lace, had Dina's neighbor wished to stare, he would have a seen a woman no longer young but agile, dressed in an oversize T-shirt and well-worn leggings, one hand vainly attempting to impose order on a nest of dark tangled curls, the other hand rubbing her generous, mobile features awake. Yawning, Dina filled her lungs to the bursting point. Despite her childhood aversion, she felt torn between remaining outdoors to sip the delicious spring air and racing inside to get a head start on her always too-full day.

She decided to give herself five minutes with the paper. Perching on the top step, Dina opened her *Chronicle* to the "Datebook" section. It was her habit to start with the comics. She never allowed herself more than a glimpse at the headlines before she read "Doonsbury," lest she be sidetracked into serious news. But a woman with her tidy habit of mind couldn't go straight for the comics page either: she had to begin with page one of the section and thumb through the reviews and celebrity gossip and horoscopes along the way.

That's where she saw the item that sent a surge of adrenalin to the roots of her hair.

Take C and See?

Leah Garchik   Wednesday, April 4, 2001

CURE FOR THE COMMON COLD? Rumor has it that under the influence of new designer drug Clarity, Warren Beatty and Michael Moore have teamed up to buy a weekly slot on the WB network to feature humor, short films and short documentaries that tell the True Stories that don't get much network airtime in these days of Big Media. Tout Hollywood is buzzing about "C," which you can't buy for love nor money: you can only get it as a gift! Is that sweet or what? So what does Clarity do? Well, according to a press release TIC received this week from a group that goes by the moniker Vitamin See, this new substance enables the user to "see through false fronts and illusions" that "obscure reality," "awakening us to what's really going on." Doesn't sound like all that much fun to TIC. Without false fronts and illusions (and let's not forget adultery and plastic surgery), yours truly would be out of a job. C's not illegal yet, darlings, so if you want to try it, look out for geeks bearing gifts—they say Silicon Valley is all aglow. Dina stood like a shot, emitting a squeal that lifted Alice's fur into the arch of a Halloween cat. Catching herself, she scanned self-consciously for any sign that she'd disturbed the neighbors, but so far as she could tell, nobody stirred. That was good, because absolutely no one could know. But if somehow they could—if security weren't the word of the day—who would possibly blame her for crowing? It was a little like getting one of those genius awards, at least as she'd always imagined it: seeing all your efforts pay off in the currency of a dream come true.

Trembling with excitement, Dina tore into the house and speed-dialed Gabe Pryor, her co-conspirator and the only real friend she had in the governor's office, even though strictly speaking, she was his boss. She raced through the flat as she talked, lugging an armful of presentable clothes to the bathroom and turning on the hot-water tap.

"Where are you?" Gabe asked, rubbing his hand from the top of his forehead to the tip of his chin and back. "I'm not even out of bed yet and it sounds like you're in a car wash. I could be way off-base here, but have you ever considered you might be taking this early-bird thing a little far?"

"'Datebook' section," said Dina commandingly, "'The In Crowd' column."

"My, we are speedy today, aren't we? No time for verbs? What's the big rush?" Gabe stumbled out of bed and made for the front door, where he hoped the paper hadn't been "borrowed" by a passerby. On the way, he caught a glimpse of himself in the mirror: same old long nose, wide on the bottom like a T-square, same old shadows around the eyes, same old too-much eyebrows, same old afterthought of a chin, giving his coffee-colored face an innocence he couldn't rightfully claim.

Dina forced herself to slow down. "Just get the paper, Gabe. I think you'll enjoy reading 'The In Crowd' today."

"Why does your voice sound so choked?" he asked. Dina was always going off about something. She e-mailed him ten times a day with one or another urgent matter, and her office was right down the hall from his.

"Because I've got the phone jammed between my neck and my shoulder and I'm trying to apply mascara one-handed while you waste my time with irrelevant questions."

"Where's the fire?"

"In the fucking 'Datebook' section," Dina told him, enunciating every syllable. She could hear the rustle of newspapers in the background now.

"Holy shit!" said Gabe, there at last. "The eagle has landed! Will you look at this! The lead item! Whoo-o-o-o!"

"The lead item," Dina repeated, dusting blusher on her cheekbones, shrugging her free shoulder philosophically when she hit the left cheek a little higher than the right.

Gabe whistled long and low. "And how long has it been? Mere weeks? I mean, I don't know who's keeping records on this stuff, and, you know, maybe nobody is, but this has to be the land-speed record for buzz."

"Three months," Dina told him, surveying her slightly lopsided lipstick. Good enough for the office. Anyway, it was usually gone by 11 o'clock: raccoon-rings around her brown eyes from forgetting not to rub them, lipstick dissolved by coffee except for a faint outline along the rim of her too-large mouth, nose shiny from the bump at its bridge to the very tip. "Three months and, um, I'd say five days, but that may not be precise."

"I'm sure the mysterious Nick has all the stats," he said. "What did your boyfriend say?"

"Nick's not my boyfriend, and anyway, I called you first." Dina felt oddly defensive about both things. "You're the first name on my speed-dial."

"Sounds like a country song," said Gabe, feeling more than a little pleased, "not that I'm an expert in such things, but hey, listen to this: 'First on my speed-dial and first in my heart…'"

"And first to break the big news." Dina squealed again; she just couldn't help it. She cadged a chorus from the Grateful Dead, slightly revised: "'What a sho-o-ort, strange trip it's been.'"

✤   ✤   ✤

Indeed, it had been remarkably short. The idea had come to Dina in January, probably helped along by too many morose New Year's conversations. Taking stock tended to depress her in those days. By the time of the year's first press conference, she was already pretty low. Closing her eyes now, she could remember her way back into those sensations, the desolate feeling of leaning against the back wall of the institutional-blue briefing room, clutching a clip-board to her chest. That January day, spooning her body around the clipboard made her think of high school: young Dina hurrying down the hallway in a stiff new back-to-school outfit, shielding her sudden breasts with a binder to ward off the greedy eyes of boys who'd awakened that summer into long, hairy, urgent bodies.

Oh my God, she'd thought, stopping herself in mid-riff to gaze around the briefing room. *How bad does reality have to be for me to prefer daydreaming about high school?*

Dina hated high school, an all-day torture chamber designed to make her feel excess to requirements: too tall, too smart, too stupid to know when to shrink and act dumb. She daydreamed through most of those years, imagining the way life would be when she was finally grown-up and free: how she could choose the people around her—they would be artists and intellectuals, it would be something like Paris in the Twenties—how she could create her own moments, make her own choices.

An electronic rattle signaled the end of her daydreams and the start of that week's press conference. Dina shook her head, inhaling the bouquet of stale coffee, trying to bring herself into sync with the present. Trying to want to be there. After all, she told herself, her girlish wishes had come remarkably close to true. As the director of this little media extravaganza, she'd created the mise en scène and scripted the main characters. Just one glitch: the resulting pro-duction made her want to run screaming from the room, never to look back.

At the podium the governor gushed charm at Barbara Hill, doyenne of the capital press corps, accessorized as always within an inch of her life. Barb reminded Dina of Mamie Eisenhower, but not many people could relate to that comparison any more. Barb had asked one of her famously direct ques-tions: "How can you raise the salaries of prison guards and the budget for new prisons when a third of our classroom teachers got layoff notices this week, and class size will climb back up to forty or more? Governor, in your last campaign you said education was going to be your number-one priority. What do you say to those pink-slipped teachers now?"

"I don't know what to say, Barb." The governor winked at a couple of amused reporters, stretching his hands toward the state and national flags that flanked the wooden podium. "I'm just so dazzled by that hat, I'm speechless." The renowned Hal Crayton smile started its slow journey to fullness, first the right corner, then the left, and finally the ranks of square white teeth standing at attention in a landscape of tan, substantial flesh, pummeling the whole room with star quality.

The governor held up his hand. "But, seriously, Barb, tough times mean tough choices. We had to trim school expenditures to balance the budget. We had no choice about that, the voters of this great state have made that a mandate. But we fought the good fight and in the end, we cut education less than other programs. That's the best anybody could hope to do under these circumstances. Education is still my first priority, just like I promised, and the voters know me as a man who keeps his promises."

Barb Hill sat forward, one hand waving like an eager student's, ready to repeat her point about prison guards. But if he knew anything, Crayton knew how to deflect tricky follow-ups—Dina had coached him hard enough to etch that lesson permanently into his memory bank. Adopting a searching air, he swiveled toward the opposite side of the room to call on a good old boy who reliably pitched him a softball.

A few more of these, and Dina felt her stomach begin to lurch in earnest. Probably that vending-machine lunch. With an upraised finger, she signaled to an aide standing in respectful silence three paces behind the governor: *One more question.* The aide signaled back with a thumb and forefinger: *Got it, just one.*

After work Dina drove straight home, heedless of the bare trees and the whistle of the January wind. She went directly to her workroom, stopping only to grab a carton of yogurt from the refrigerator. Spooning up sweet pink blandness, she peered at the computer screen. Alice occupied her accustomed perch behind the monitor, one gray, furry leg straight in the air as she enthusiastically licked her butt. Dina tried not to take it as a feline reproach, but she was neck-deep into self-reproof anyway, so there was no point resisting. *My magnum opus,* she thought, *my unfinished symphony. My black hole.*

Dina had begun the film in question a full seven years earlier, the same month she'd taken her job with the newly elected Governor Crayton. "To keep myself honest," she'd said at the time. But she hadn't really meant it, feeling complacently sure that nothing could tempt her to stray from the path of integrity. The real point of starting the film had been to inoculate herself against losing the creativity and independence she'd achieved as a filmmaker. She'd imagined it as a simple trade-off: the steady paycheck would buy her time, and she'd use it to make "If I Am For Myself Alone," her exploration of the great questions of empathy in human events.

A wise teacher had once advised her to set the course for any project by committing its essence to paper in just a few sentences, consulting it frequently to make sure everything she did advanced her stated aims. The smudged and ragged scrap of paper had been taped to her computer forever. Its two sentences read this way:

> How do we come to feel connection, the kind that leads to cooperation and altruism? And how do we come to feel its opposite, that other people are merely things blocking our path?

Dina's approach to her film's subject was to examine figures in history, both those who transcended their own origins and crude self-interest to become heroes of liberty, and those who turned their backs on the world's suffering, devoted only to serving themselves. Dina believed in underlying truth. She was sure that by examining reality with an open mind and heart, one could discern the skeleton—the armature, the way things really worked, the machinery of cause and effect—beneath the thick skin of evasion, denial, rationalization.

But after seven years, all she had was a slew of sections that hadn't yet cohered into a film—Moses giving up his royal privilege to smite the overseer oppressing the Hebrews, Che Guevara in the mountains of Bolivia, Eleanor Roosevelt's embrace of the underdog...Examining any of these lives, she could draw lines from a certain influence in childhood to a particular adult choice, and it would all look perfectly logical. But it was usually easy to find someone else with a similar childhood who'd chosen the opposite path: a vicious bully sires two sons, one who follows in his footsteps and another who rescues abused children. With the security of hindsight, it was easy to cook up causalities, stirring a dollop of psychology into fragments of biography. But Dina's old science teacher taught that to be valid, a theory couldn't just serve as a plausible description of the way things have behaved in the past; it must predict how they will behave in future. The bippety-boppety-boo of psychological theory didn't seem to possess much predictive power. In the end, what *made* people what they were, Dina just didn't know.

Yeah, yeah. Alice's indifferent licking seemed to say Dina's stories weren't likely to hang together anytime soon if all she did was give the film her leftover energy after another day of media spin and manipulation.

Along with her yogurt, Dina was chewing on the theory that the main obstacle to her own creativity might be the chaos in her immediate surroundings. Like the rest of her flat, the décor of her workroom was graduate-student bricks-and-boards meets IKEA: a rather nice computer desk next to a table made from an old door propped on sawhorses, half-dead flowers in a Mason jar, pens and pencils in a hi-tech wire mesh holder. While she tried to keep her more public rooms tidy, the workroom was almost impassable, years' worth of film cans moldering in a corner, blocking access to shelves crammed with reference books, grant guidelines, file folders of notes and treatments and budgets.

Her footage had been transferred to digital video a few years back, and now most nights found Dina in a corner of this chaos, slouching at the keyboard, trying to make sense of it all. Her computer was surrounded by a veritable fairyland of LEDs, each one twinkling a slightly different time—blue numbers on the radio and telephone, red for the tape deck and VCR—but right now, all the colors said it was sometime after midnight. Sighing, letting the room go out of focus, Dina rubbed her forehead. No need to be terribly bright-eyed in the morning. She'd let herself have until 12:30 tonight. She brought up the file labeled "Gandhi" and let it unspool, a rough assemblage of old newsreel footage, Gandhi's greatest hits.

The large brown bald head, the leathery ears, the skinny neck and shoulders no bigger than a ten year-old's—Dina's eyes filled with that sweet variety of tears evoked by baby pictures and canyon sunsets. She had read that Gandhi studied law in England, practiced it in South Africa. It was as if Dr. Martin Luther King had abandoned his title and business suits in favor of dusty overalls and a hoe—so unlikely and so humble and so incredibly shrewd.

"To a people famishing and idle," the Gandhi on Dina's computer screen said, "the only acceptable form in which God can dare appear is work and promise of food as wages."

Dina hit "pause." The radio playing softly in the background came into her awareness. "At 9:15 GMT," the plummy British voice said, "we have Angus Mitchell from Baghdad reporting on the situation of the Kurds today, followed by Joan Childers from Hong Kong, where a mysterious ailment thought to be flu is turning out to be a by-product of industrial pollution, and then to Sean McDonald in Hollywood, where the latest craze is designer water—no, not

Perrier nor Evian, but bottled water individually tailored to the stars' elec-
trolytes by a computer program designed for that purpose."

"To a people in a trance of consumerism and indifference," Dina said, mim-
icking Gandhi's inflection, "the only acceptable form in which God can dare
appear is as a new drug." She rubbed the underside of Alice's chin, caressing the
cat's tiny bones. "Just blow their minds and wake them up," she told the
purring kitty.

Dina glanced at the old photo of Nick propped behind the clock: the excel-
lent bones, clear light eyes and straight-falling fair hair. Despite decades
devoted to perfecting his bad habits—Nick must have been nearly forty when
this picture was taken—he retained that English schoolboy look, a sensuous
innocence that hooked Dina like a fish. She kept meaning to put the picture
away. It had a sticky quality, drawing her eyes when all she'd wanted was to
know the time, then entrapping her into a silent conversation with Nick's fad-
ing image.

Lately, the main conversation topic was resentment. *I wasted my youth on
you*, Dina told Nick's black-and-white gaze, bitter bile rising in her throat. To
be fair, she hadn't exactly thrown away her life: she'd learned to be a filmmaker,
made her way in the world, had fun, made a difference. But now she was a
forty-six-fucking-year-old workaholic, no family, no man, no predictable
future. All the time most people invested in getting those things, she'd squan-
dered on a complicated trip around the block with Nick Emerson, *puer aeter-
nis*—the eternal youth, as her friend Ronnie the shrink explained, a Jungian
archetype for seductive, charismatic men who never grow up. Yet whenever
one of Dina's well-meaning friends persuaded her to have dinner with a cousin
or colleague who would be "perfect for you, just perfect," she defeated herself
hoping for the instant ease, the mutual comprehension she'd felt with Nick at
their best. Was the enduring bruise on her heart Nick's fault, or Dina's punishment for forgetting to duck? She stared into the unchanging eyes and felt that
stab again, the soreness that wouldn't heal.

For just a second, Nick's photo seemed to glow in the dark, especially his
Cheshire cat smile. Dina felt a rumble somewhere deep inside, nothing like
pain. She made a point of ignoring it—a touch of indigestion, perhaps, but
Alice, who missed nothing, stopped purring and said "O-w-w-w-l!" This was
her cry to signal any change in the atmosphere. "Owl," whispered Dina,
stroking the cat's soft fur. "Owl and owl again."

❦   ❦   ❦

Trapped in her seat at the governor's conference table a couple of days later, Dina had a sensation that was all too familiar yet very difficult to describe without resorting to outlandish analogies. Her limbs felt strained and congested, like sausages cooked nearly to the bursting point. She'd choked down a quantity of frustration so enormous it had migrated from the realm of thought and speech into a crude bodily sensation, the muscular equivalent of having to vomit. She yearned to make a sound—a kvetch, a screech, a grunt—an utterance more basic than speech, more primitive than thought. She wanted so much to drop under the table and pound the floor with her arms and legs in time with her groans, it was taking one hundred percent of her will to restrain the impulse.

That was probably a good thing, because it left her no energy to say what she thought, which was that the entire senior staff and cabinet of Governor Hal Crayton's administration was so debased, so deluded, so detached from what it meant to be human and from the responsibilities that entailed—so clueless they might as well lie down and die.

Encased in self-imposed silence, Dina simmered inside her sausage skin, watching the simulacra do their thing: smiling and nodding around the long polished wood table, their mouths moving against a backdrop of velvet curtains, formal portraits. Every so often, one of them would point or wave in her direction, then continue yapping without even waiting to see if she had acknowledged the gesture. Gabe sneaked glances at her, sidewise and anxious, as if he was waiting for her to go off like a stick of dynamite. She had absolutely no idea what they were all talking about now.

The morning's featured dumb show had focused on commercialization of public education. Dina had been quietly advising a coalition of parents' and educators' groups that had been working to prohibit commercial messages from being broadcast in classrooms. Constituent work wasn't part of her job description, but occasionally—more than occasionally, if truth be told—some friend of a bleeding-heart friend would get to her and more often than not, she found herself swept away with the injustice of it all and scheduling a meeting.

This particular campaign was dropped on her desk by Ronnie, whose therapy practice was mostly with children. If successful, it would do away with Channel One and with "VNRs"—video news releases, pre-packaged "news stories" or "documentaries" underwritten by advertisers. The parents had shown her one on students' back problems sponsored by a backpack manufacturer and another on the African American "Juneteenth" holiday sponsored by a meat company whose products featured prominently in footage of celebratory barbecues. If they succeeded in ridding the classroom of commercial messages, they'd move on to other corporate exploitation of children, like school districts turning their cafeterias over to McDonald's or Pizza Hut.

You had to admire the corporations' talent for enterprise: Channel One and the fast-food outlets had a real feel for commercial synergy. Students got to see the McDonald's logo and food in the underwriting credits during second or third period, for instance, then, when the lunch bell rang, they could run to the cafeteria to satisfy the high-fat, high-sugar cravings thus created. The schools got money, the corporations made money, and as no one cared all that much about the collateral damage, everyone who really mattered was happy.

These practices had been so widely accepted, they'd become normalized. Dina hadn't really gotten the magnitude of the problem until one mother of a "tweener" (that was the corporations' target demographic, nine-to-fourteen–year-olds whose consumer habits were just being formed) came to her office, outraged almost beyond words. Like most of Ronnie's referrals, the woman bore the signs of having done serious time in the counterculture: wavy graying hair that showed no evidence of having been gelled and teased or otherwise tortured; natural fibers, clear blue eyes set in a net of sun-etched lines.

"I don't know how to make you people understand," the woman had said.

"You people" had stung, Dina had to admit that. "How about let's try," she asked, "before giving up?"

The woman looked briefly startled, then launched into her tale. "My son Adam is nine," she told Dina, "and one of the kindest, most trusting people you could ever meet. He's smart too, and remembers just about everything he learns. He doesn't watch much television, and we're very careful about the few things we allow him to watch." She waited for Dina's nod of acknowledgement. "He loves school, at least most of it. It's important to me that he feel safe in that environment, that his trust is justified. Do you get that?" She'd looked at Dina as if she were a big dog who might not have the brainpower to understand the command "Stay!"

Dina choked back her resentment and nodded again.

"One day, I asked Adam what he had learned in school and when he answered me it was like *The Exorcist* or something. He recited all this ad copy verbatim, feeling very proud of himself. 'Did you know, Mommy, that scooters are safer than skateboards? They provide the most transportation value for the dollar. Did you know that everybody needs to drink three glasses of milk each day? Did you know that if you want to have healthy feet they need a 75,000-mile checkup from a podiatrist?' Only Adam said 'potriadist.' Then he asked me if he could get McDonald's for lunch the next day."

The mother ran her hands through her hair, sighing. "I asked him if it was okay to believe everything he saw on TV, and that was obviously a brand-new question. I went to see his teacher. She sat there, bold as brass, telling me that with so many things competing for priority, there wasn't any time to talk about these claims." The woman's voice began to rise. "She actually tried to calm me down by assuring me that she held a pop quiz every so often to find out if the students retained what they'd learned from Channel One!"

Dina winced. This was so crazy. Didn't people realize what they were doing by selling their kids to corporate America? Suddenly, incongruously, she saw herself sitting cross-legged, draped in white homespun, pronouncing her wacky version of Gandhi's wisdom: *To a people in a trance of consumerism and indifference, the only acceptable form in which God can dare appear is as a new drug.*

"Ms. Meyer, are you listening to me?" Clearly annoyed, the woman stared at Dina.

"Sorry," said Dina, shaking her head. "What you're telling me is shocking. Please, go on."

"So I took it to the PTA," the outraged mother continued. "Everybody was with me. How could they mess with kids' minds and bodies this way? And all these teachers' groups are against it. And everybody tells me the governor is the one who can change it. So how can we get to him, Ms. Meyer? Because these people are messing with my son, and I'm not going to just sit here and take that!"

At home that night, Dina couldn't get this conversation out of her mind. It wasn't as if this was the biggest issue in the world, but in a way, that made it worse. As far as she could see, most of those who should have been responsible for protecting children's welfare (not to mention the well-being of adults, animals, trees and rivers) were asleep on the job. It was as if someone really had put them into a trance, like hypnotic subjects in a stage act. If only there really could be a drug that would make people see through the trance, she'd gladly add it to the water supply. She tossed and turned all night, awakened a dozen times by the same thoughts.

The next day, for the first cabinet and senior-staff meeting of the new year, Dina brought the issue to the table, certain it deserved a fair hearing—and hoping that a few days off for the holidays might have cleared some of the cobwebs from her colleagues' vision. But neither facts nor arguments had outweighed simple dollars and cents.

This was explained to Dina at a pace and in a tone that suggested she was an imbecile to not understand it for herself. Didn't she realize that Channel One was a free service, replacing costly curriculum? Turning the cafeteria over to Pizza Hut slashed the budget for food and food-service personnel. This was public-private cooperation, a fine thing for everyone, especially the taxpayer. Alan Bridge, the balding, avuncular head of Food and Agriculture, sealed the deal by chiming in that McDonald's had promised to use in-state suppliers of meat and produce.

"And besides," he said, rubbing his ample stomach, "who doesn't like to have a Big Mac and fries now and then?"

Gandhi rose slowly into Dina's field of vision. She quickly shook him to the back of her mind.

"Oh," said Kathy Nakano, head of the Department of Alcohol and Drug Programs, looking uncharacteristically dreamy. "Wouldn't you miss Salisbury steak, whatever that was? With carrot sticks and Jell-o, in those trays with compartments." She fingered the bow on her white blouse.

"Yeah," said Alan, caught up in the fun, "what would you rather have, a Big Mac or Sloppy Joes? We got them once a week. I had a friend who said they looked like pre-eaten hamburgers."

"E-e-e-w!" groaned Marian Jason, the governor's executive assistant. "Thanks for the imagery."

Everyone chuckled and nodded like bobblehead dolls while Dina, who'd just read the reviews of the newly published *Fast Food Nation*, bit her tongue from repeating her friend Nancy's line on the subject: "You've *got* to read it. There's shit in the meat!"

"Look," said Dina, "it's really very simple. If you would just open your eyes, I'm sure you would see it for yourselves. Shouldn't school balance all the TV commercials kids are getting at home, instead of reinforcing them? Don't we have a higher educational purpose than selling Big Macs?"

"What?" said Bob Bornstein, the head of the Technology, Trade & Commerce Agency. He usually looked like an insurance agent, colorless and dull. But when he was irked, his complexion took on the color of rare beef, and then Dina thought he looked menacing. "Fomenting class warfare? Why is it you always object if anyone but the taxpayer foots the bill? Where could we get the money to feed these students if McDonald's pulled out? By raising taxes?"

Dina had been typecast, of that there was no doubt. She felt like an idiot for even imagining that what she had to say would be considered on its merits. Gabe was at the meeting just to report on one issue. He was keeping his head down, seemingly intent on something fascinating in a file folder, but Dina guessed he was paying attention, because he was using all of his body language to telegraph the message she should let it go. But Dina couldn't seem to help herself. She opened her mouth to try again.

"Okay," said the governor preemptively, raising his hand to signal a timeout. "Enough. I agree with my principled friend Dina. I'd like to be able to run the schools the old-fashioned way. But it's impossible. We can't afford it, and I'm not going to dump this problem on my successor either."

"But," Dina started, "what about the millions for prison...."

"Now you sound like Barb Hill," Crayton said, lips bending into a tight little smile. There was laughter all around. He shifted his gaze up one side of the big conference table and down the other, making the briefest eye contact with each person. Silence descended.

Throughout the rest of the meeting, Dina doodled on her notepad, trying to cool herself down. But every time her breathing returned to normal, she remembered what she would have to say to the outraged mother and her friends: *Sorry, folks, the great state of California is going to continue selling your kids to the highest bidder, just as long as it pays. But don't worry, we're building more prisons to hold the results.* She found herself sketching a figure that resembled Gandhi in the film clip, large, round head atop bird bones, wrapped in a white sheet.

The only acceptable form in which God can dare appear is as a new drug.

If only that were possible...

The photo of Nick popped onto the screen of Dina's memory-bank. She pushed it away, but it popped right up again. He might have treated her badly, but this wasn't personal. It was much bigger than that, and Nick was unquestionably the go-to guy. Dina couldn't live with herself if she let a bruised heart stand in the way of what might be possible after all. Where had she put his number?

❦   ❦   ❦

Nick was up at first light, bustling around the house, moving to the soundtrack of his own self-disparagement. People always talked about an "inner dialogue," but for Nick, it was a monologue. There didn't seem to be room for two voices in his head.

Right, man, it said, *whatever bullshit she told you about needing your "expertise" for a new idea, it's just a cover story. Yeah, she's madly in love with you, ready to rush back to you, she's just been postponing it for seven years 'cause she was a little busy.*

Bend over, the voice said, *because she's going to kick your ass. But be sure to get the place real neat first, 'cause that's so important, making a good impression while you get creamed.*

Nick sighed, checking his face in the mirror. Seven years. He knew he looked okay. He had one of those faces that were supposed to age well. Good bone structure, his barber always said. More lines, more gray, but he was in decent shape. He could still set his sights on a woman in a bar and nine times out of ten, she'd let him join her at her table while she sipped the drink he'd bought, giggling at his jokes.

Yeah, said the voice. *That's where you met all those Mother Teresas and Nobel Prize-winners, huh?*

Nick spooned tea into a hinged mesh ball and plopped it into the blue teapot. For seven years, he'd evaded thoughts of Dina. They'd lurked at the edge of his awareness like the phantom pain amputees suffered in the legs they'd lost. When he felt a twinge, he pushed it to the back of his mind. But the second he'd heard Dina's voice on the phone, his old pain had blossomed into flesh. Now she was coming here on some errand he hadn't quite understood—reminding him of that Berryman poem his father always used to quote: "His mission was real, but obscure." She probably thought of him as "good old Nick." She probably felt enough time had passed, that they could meet like old pals and part again as easily.

Each thought tightened the knot in Nick's stomach. He put his hands over the knot and sat on the couch to wait.

Nick didn't put too much stock in people. In principle, he couldn't buy this idea of soul mates, the notion that you were meant to be teamed up with someone else for life. It seemed weak and dangerous—yoked at the hip, like his parents, hobbling along, forgetting why. But when he looked back on everything, he had to admit it, the one good thing he'd done, the one thing that was wildly, totally worth doing—like grabbing a life preserver—was hook up with Dina, his heart's desire.

Get ready for her to be old and tired, the voice said, *like some burnt-out schoolteacher. Or married. Or both.*

Sighing, Nick opened his laptop, preparing to check his e-mail while he waited. He wished he didn't feel he was waiting for some test results or the return of a jury.

❦   ❦   ❦

Driving at tortoise speed up the rocky curving track, Dina remembered. Seven years was a long time. She felt nervous, like a girl on a first date. But that was absurd. Even if this visit hadn't been strictly business, it was ridiculous to think in romantic terms about Nick Emerson, a man she'd known since college. The man she'd lived with until she decided to take the Sacramento job and he'd asked how she planned to explain to the folks doing the security check that her boyfriend was a drug dealer. The man she now regaled with her resentment almost every night—in absentia.

They hadn't exactly broken up, more faded away. At first the change in their arrangement had been an appearances-only thing: they'd live apart, but still see each other. Then it was convenience. Nick bought the land to build this place, and commuting from Sonoma County to Sacramento was out of the question for Dina. After a year or so, their visits had become so few and far between, the relationship just petered out.

They hadn't talked at all for years—not since a highly unpleasant phone call at the start of Crayton's second campaign. Dina thought "media whore" was an inapt and extreme characterization of her job, and Nick hadn't much liked it when she'd accused him of hiding in an ivory armchair like his father, finding fault with the Lilliputians who made up the human race. And now she had come to ask for his help. Was she nuts?

Dina stopped the car and peered at her face in the rear view mirror. The things about it that made her self-conscious—wild hair, too much mouth, eyes like Dondi—those had been what Nick professed to love. She moistened a finger and ran it under her eyes, wiping away the smeared mascara. She decided not to refresh her lipstick. That would look eager, and that was the last thing she wanted.

"I would have left a trail of breadcrumbs," Dina said brightly, "but I thought the squirrels would get them."

Nick leaned against the doorjamb, head to one side, looking her over. The clothes were a little aging-preppy, not like the old days. But she was still Dina, that energy crackling off her tangled hair, the liquid brown eyes taking it all in. *Not burnt-out*, he told the voice. He glanced at her left hand. *And not married.* "It's almost impossible to get lost on the way out," he said to Dina. "You just keep going down."

"I thought I might get to come in first." Nick having moved an inch or so to the side, Dina slid through the doorway, not quite touching him, but smelling him, yes, that familiar, elusive running-water scent that said *Nick*.

The place was gorgeous, she had to hand him that. The house seemed to have grown *in situ* like a mushroom, rather than deriving from the usual business of plans and timbers, hammers and saws and nails. There were very few square corners or straight angles, just polished wood curving with the grain, making her want to reach out and stroke the walls. Across the room, a vast picture window opened onto an extraordinary prospect, the sun coming up over hills covered in the improbably green grass of a northern California winter. Oaks dotted the hillsides, chamise and manzanita clung to the ground: the prickly native plants of her native state, surviving more on the memory of water than its actuality.

"Tea on the porch?" Nick asked, hands in his pockets. He wanted to lay his fingers close to Dina's scalp and tug softly, see if that still made her purr.

Dina felt pleased to accept a steaming cup, pleased that Nick had gone to the trouble of setting out the pot and cups and the little plate of cut-up fruit in anticipation of her arrival—and she was quick to push that pleasure to the back of her awareness. "You're probably wondering why I called you," said Dina, sipping her tea, still unsure how to go about explaining, but certain she had come on an errand, not a quest.

"I guess I thought you got a yearning to sit in an ivory armchair," Nick replied, wearing that lopsided grin, patting his lap, impersonating ease.

Dina felt her cheeks go red. "Or just needed a break from media whoring?"

"Touché."

Both of them felt the old buzz, the familiar pleasure of sparring together, and both suppressed it before the feeling could take root. The sun crowned over the far hills, slicing the air with a powerful beam. Dina and Nick shielded their eyes, like a team of scouts gazing toward a distant shore, the fair one appearing composed, the other dark and rattled, unmistakably rattled.

Dina took a deep breath, plunging ahead, getting down to business. "Have you got a VCR?"

She showed him the Gandhi footage and shared her insight about God appearing as a new drug. At first Nick thought it was a joke, but Dina persevered.

"The world is going to hell in a handbasket, Nick."

That crooked smile still made him look debonair, like a man in an old snapshot, sporting the fedora and cigarette of another age. "Nice handbasket," he said, narrowing his blue eyes to slits, pretending to admire the handicraft that had produced this imaginary merchandise. "I could unload a couple gross of those."

Resisting the bait, Dina continued. "Things are pretty fucked up, wouldn't you agree?" She rubbed her eyes and waited.

"Well, yes. I believe I may have made that point sometime in 1978." *And again in '79, '80, '81….*

"Yes, well, things were fucked up in '78, but wouldn't you agree that they've reached a point that lends new meaning to 'fucked up'?" Dina waited for Nick's nod, and eventually it came. "It seems like everyone is in some kind of trance." She could see him getting that smug smirk on his face, that I-told-you-so expression, but she tried not to let it throw her. "Nick," she said, all seriousness now, brown eyes huge, lips set, "it doesn't matter who said it first. It doesn't matter who was right. This is beyond that."

"Did you quit your job?" he asked. "Or is this one of those I-have-met-the-enemy-and-he-is-us kind of things? Getting all worked up while you work the system?" He'd forgotten about this part, the way self-righteousness leaked into their exchanges, their famous point-counterpoints. In retrospect, it didn't seem like all that much fun.

What's the matter, baby? asked Nick's inner voice. *Feeling disappointed that she's not throwing herself at you?*

"You could put it that way," Dina said, stifling her dismay. Were they going to revert instantly to some old pissing match? "Or you could say that I have tried to work within the system, so my desire to take another road at this point is grounded in sad experience. Or maybe if I just said I spent an entire morning listening to the cream of our public service convince themselves that broadcasting commercials into classrooms and turning cafeterias over to McDonald's was a win-win proposition, and I'm fresh out of patience." She sat quietly, waiting for him to speak.

Nick put down his tea, finally ready to listen. So what if Dina didn't come to throw herself at him? This could be interesting. He gestured for her to continue.

"Politics is lost, because it's all about money and lies," said Dina, feeling her face grow warm. "Sometimes I wonder if politics is even going to matter anymore compared to the multinationals." Dina could hear the hysteria creeping into her voice, but desperate to convince Nick, she ignored it and pushed on. "People's lives are just numbers now in this big globalization game, the whole world is their plaything. Meanwhile, back at the ranch, we've been assimilated by the shopping culture: life is what you want to buy, identity is what you own, kids' whole frame of reference is manufactured somewhere in Hollywood.

"I sit in front of my computer all day, so maybe that is narrowing my vision. But I keep thinking the only thing that can help us now is something that wakes people up deep, down inside, in the place where our ability to understand the world is formed. Like in a computer: we don't need a bunch of fancy new software bells and whistles. We need to repair our operating system."

Nick nodded. This fire was one of the things he'd always loved about Dina, how she cared so passionately about the world, how she actually thought about how to fix it. "Go on," he said.

"So that's it, what I said." She shrugged, her mouth curving into a half-smile. "We need a new drug, and I want to know if it can be done. Naturally, I thought I'd come to the source."

CHAPTER 2

Seeing Nick Emerson set Dina to reminiscing. Nick was such a creature of his times. At Berkeley in the Seventies, everyone had seen him as the cutting-edge of cool, always ahead of the curve. He looked like a star, everybody thought so: his hair falling just so across the tops of his amber-tinted shades, the chiseled cheeks and chin, the pale mouth hovering halfway between amusement and arrogance. Whatever he did was instantly copied. In critique class, Nick's wry, drawling style of commentary became the lingua franca, just as his taste in sunglasses established the standard. His student films seemed so original, so startling at first. But a few months after he'd done something, you would see it echoed everywhere, as if he were setting the agenda for the next big thing.

At first, Dina had been turned off. "He's a college sophomore," she told her roommate, "not James Dean." But then he'd captured her heart by comparing one of her earliest efforts to the work of Maya Deren, removing his shades to emphasize the point with an intensely blue gaze. She began to think he might be James Dean after all. To take the edge off her adoration, Dina used to tease Nick about riding the wave of what's cool. Holding an imaginary microphone to his chin, she pretended to be a TV interviewer. "Let's find out what Mr. Zeitgeist thinks about that," she'd say brightly. "Tell us, Mr. Z."

Nick had always batted the imaginary mike away, expressing his disdain for the actual-existing media. He'd come by that hauteur early, at his father's knee.

Nick's dad Robert (never Bob or Rob or Bobby) taught contemporary English literature at Columbia. Although his world was almost entirely circumscribed by the Upper West Side corridor between the family's dark, book-lined apartment on Riverside Drive and his cluttered office on campus, Robert had been certain it was the center of the universe, affording an especially fine and sweeping view. He had an opinion on everything, and it was usually the same opinion: he deemed most things rather second-rate. He was always first with a verdict on a writer no one had heard of, just before the name began to pop up in papers and journals. He knew the best Scotch and the best bookstore and the best place to buy the good English cheddar and cream crackers his wife Peg subsisted on, and with few exceptions, he also found the rest of the world very easy to know and to dismiss.

The first time Nick brought Dina home, it had been winter break. The pair had been inseparable since that film critique class. They went to all the out-of-the-way screenings of obscure films. They smoked dope and dreamed out loud about all the films they were going to make, how they would change the world. Nick loved to move his fingers along Dina's scalp, caressing her curls. He outlined her lips with his thumb, telling her that she was the embodiment of his longing as a child, to have dark curly hair and a folk dance, he said, an ethnicity other than WASP. They studied together, or rather pretended to study while touching legs and hands under the library table until they couldn't stand it, until it became imperative to race back to Nick's place, throwing off their clothes on the way to the rumpled mattress.

Nick didn't think taking Dina home for the holidays was such a great idea, but she'd insisted. In truth, she found herself gripped by the suburban Jewish kid's inchoate longing to experience an authentic WASP Christmas with snow-drifts and eggnog and a fragrant green tree in the living room. Besides, she'd never been to New York, and she'd seen real winter, complete with snow, only a couple of times, on trips to Tahoe. Nick had laughed at her fantasies, but in the end, he'd succumbed to the argument that going away together meant they could sleep in the same bed every night.

At 8:30 on Christmas Eve, loopy from a tumbler brimful of Scotch and starving on nothing but cheese and crackers, Dina had pulled Nick into his father's study to complain.

"I tried to tell you," he said, raking back his light hair, aiming his blue eyes at the overstuffed bookcases, the worn Turkish carpet, everywhere but at Dina. This was—had been—predictable. On the whole, Nick thought families were a bad idea. Too much vulnerability mixed with too much disappointment. His notion of a perfect visit home was seeing Robert and Peg at breakfast a couple of times, the watercress-thin filling in a bready sandwich of bookstores, films, bars and coffeehouses, hanging out with friends.

Dina felt the room shift as a new perspective came into focus. "Yes," she wailed, "but I thought you were just being ironic and understated." No chestnuts roasting on an open fire, he'd said. No Christmas goose. No Tiny Tim. His parents liked to show they were above plebeian things like Christmas. In Dina's imagination, such descriptions evoked the height of glamorous sophistication:

Celeste Holm in taupe taffeta with a wasp waist, laughing musically at Cary Grant's arch cocktail conversation while the banal world nibbled candy canes. But Robert Emerson resembled a blond Abraham Lincoln, leathery and dry with long folded legs that reminded Dina of a praying mantis. And Peg Emerson in the flesh was less like a movie star than a sturdy little dog, with her short, round nose and bright eyes, her hair graying at the temples and her barking laugh. After her third giant Scotch Peg seemed uninterested even in the plate of orange cheese and thick white crackers. Each time she spoke, her words were a little slower and more precise than the time before. There was no smell of cooking from the kitchen.

After Dina's rude awakening, she and Nick had gone out for pizza. The next morning, all four of them had jammed into the breakfast nook for a meal of heavily alcoholic eggnog, black coffee, and English muffins with marmalade. Neither parent made mention of the young people's absence the night before. Everyone was given a section of the *New York Times,* and the only conversation came from Nick's parents reading aloud snippets of news and gossip that supported the family's sense of superiority—or at least the idea that everyone else was brainless and inept. Nick's Christmas present had been a big check—Dina saw three zeros over his shoulder when he opened the envelope—and hers had been a tiny bottle of Chanel No. 5, pre-wrapped at the store in colored cellophane with a gold seal. When she'd gone to kiss Nick's mother thank you, Peg had turned her face away. Dina felt hurt until she saw the same reflexive gesture deflecting Nick's good-bye kiss. *Don't take it personally* became her mantra for their infrequent visits to Riverside Drive.

They returned to Berkeley via Dina's family home in a suburb of San Francisco. The Milners' tract house looked smaller than ever in fresh comparison with the Emersons' apartment on Riverside Drive. *At least the great Hanukkah extravaganza is over,* Dina thought, sparing Nick the sight of all the clever decorations her mother had first devised to convince the kids Jews weren't missing anything by not celebrating Christmas.

Charlotte was handy in a Fifties housewife sort of way: she could tighten a nut or replace a plug, and she loved to occupy herself with little craft projects, appliquéing gingham cut-outs on towels, teaching Dina's Brownies troop to decorate matchbooks with glitter. For Hanukkah, she had traced menorah shapes onto Styrofoam and trimmed them with swathes of bright blue glitter, attaching a small blue flame-shaped light to the top of each "candle." These sat in the window every winter, glowing each night to let the neighbors know the Milner family was Jewish and proud of it. There was a long blue-and-silver festoon spelling out "Happy Hanukkah" that Charlotte stretched every winter across the archway between the living room and dining room. There were even trailing royal blue and silver tassels made out of the stuff that people flung onto their Christmas trees to simulate icicles, and dreidl-shaped cookies with blue icing and silver dragées. (Dina's dad had once confided that as a new bride, Charlotte staved off the prospect of boredom at the dining table by dyeing the food with vegetable coloring: pink mashed potatoes, purple soup). Wondering what Peg and Robert Emerson would have made of it all, Dina gave thanks that the decorations had been packed away before her arrival, so she wouldn't have to deal with even Nick's reaction this year.

Unable to contain her excitement, Charlotte Milner spilled onto the sidewalk to greet Dina and Nick as they got out of the car. Plump and lacquered, cozy in a beaded cardigan and ruffled apron layered over her dress, it was easy to see why she loved to be told she resembled Ava Gardner. She kissed Dina, then took Nick's face between her hands and turned it side to side, like a canny buyer scrutinizing a melon. "Such a handsome face," she said to Dina, as if Nick were absent, or merely deaf. "Such dimples." Charlotte took a lock of Nick's long blond hair in each hand. "But he's got to cut this hair, you can't see how gorgeous he is with all this stuff in the way." Nick looked stunned, like a deer in the headlights.

Bernie was waiting just inside, hands in pockets, bow tie crisp, slightly sheepish in his crewcut way. He shook hands with Nick, testing the boy's grip. When he hugged Dina, he whispered, "Good handshake, I can tell he's a mensch. Even if he's not Jewish." Bernie's ambition was to be the perfect dad, like *Father Knows Best* on television. Dina could feel him twinkling with a goodwill that verged on desperation, squeezing out sparks.

Dina thought this must be because Bernie's own father had been so extravagantly imperfect. Grandpa—David Milner—could never have been played by Robert Young. Charlotte always said he looked like Jeff Chandler, the Jewish movie star (cast as a gypsy, an Indian, even a passionate WASP, but never a Jew): tight gray curls, chiseled cheekbones, soulful eyes, sensuously curving mouth, muscles shifting beneath the starched white cotton. David had been a rake, a boxer, a gambler, living by his grace and wit and spending every dime as soon as he made it.

Charlotte had adored David, sitting at his feet for hours, mesmerized by his tales of adventure and risk while Bernie busied himself in the next room, pretending to work, wanting the visit to be over. When they came along, Dina and Deb took turns sitting on Grandpa's knee, Dina keeping one nervous eye on her Daddy, not wanting him to feel slighted. After David left, Bernie would always explain that his father was romanticizing times that had been terribly hard on a small boy, moving from place to place, never putting down roots. Disloyally, Charlotte nevertheless continued to find her father-in-law delicious, and Dina easily acquired her mother's taste for the type. But Deb had been happy to be Daddy's girl, so in the end, things worked out. David was so much the opposite of Charlotte's own stern, withdrawn father—hugging Zaydie had been like trying to cuddle with a tree, Dina remembered—it sometimes seemed as if Charlotte and Dina had cobbled him together with Styrofoam and glitter to satisfy their own paternal needs.

Now, for Nick's visit, Deb was sleeping over at a friend's (albeit under protest) and Bernie was shoehorning himself into character as the interested, caring father. Not a stretch, really—he *did* care, he *was* interested—just a little stiffer than if he had allowed himself to be himself rather than merely acting the part. To balance his wooden quality, Charlotte turned up the warmth, cocking one eyebrow rakishly, ready to entertain and charm the kids.

Bernie asked Nick a raft of questions about school—his major, his plans— as if he were completing a job application checklist. Dina, trying to make a dent in the slab of pot roast on her plate, silently prayed that something would interrupt the interrogative flow before her father got to how many children Nick wanted. Nick wasn't the type of man who planned such things, anyway. Her father would probably be surprised to know that she wasn't that type of woman, either.

Charlotte supplied the interruption. "Bernie," she chided, as if chastising a child, "let the young man eat. He hasn't been able to take a bite with all these questions."

Dina's sigh of relief was cut short when her mother turned the attention her way. "So," Charlotte asked, "did you have a nice visit with Nicky's parents?"

Nicky? Nick grabbed Dina's hand under the table and squeezed hard. She knew what it meant: *Don't worry, I can take it, and besides, this too shall pass.* But it took as long to pass as a kidney stone. The Emersons' indifference had been hard to take, but now Dina found herself wondering whether the Milners' attentions were more trying. First she and Nick had to eat more food than either of them normally consumed in a week. Then Dina endured the embarrassment of watching her parents collapse into their favorite chairs, clutching their stomachs and groaning, the sign of a truly great meal chez Milner. Dina and Nick refused a second piece of cake "to wash it down."

Later, Charlotte perched on the arm of the sofa, stroking Dina's dark curls as she told Nick how proud they were of their brilliant and beautiful girl.

"Although we hope she'll give up this movie business and settle on something sensible," Bernie added, "maybe teaching." He had thirty years at Kaiser, and he couldn't ask for a better job, or better benefits, or a nicer bunch of guys. He tried to be flexible. Women wanted to work nowadays, and if that's what Dina wanted, "It should be something secure."

When Nick nodded politely, Charlotte exclaimed, "See, darling! He agrees with Daddy!"

Dina couldn't help imagining what Nick must be thinking: *So déclassé, so excessive, so all over each other.* He had that anthropological expression on his face, the one that said "So this is how the creatures on this planet live," the one that most resembled his father. But when they got back into the car and Dina groaned, prepared for a good long kvetch, all Nick had said was, "At least they love you."

Thinking about the Emersons, she had to agree. At least they did.

❦   ❦   ❦

That next summer, the last before Dina's senior year, Nick graduated. He rented a house in Stinson Beach, a few steps from the Pacific, a stucco box with chilly linoleum floors. Nick hung the seafoam green walls with posters and pieces of weaving that clashed mightily with the Indian bedspreads tossed onto lumpy sofas and armchairs. Candles dripped rainbows onto the necks of green glass wine bottles. Dried flowers molted in milk jugs. There was sand in everything, on everything, and that sweet salty smell of skin too long in the sun. Sometimes Nick and Dina took a blanket out onto the dunes and made love. She liked to reach one arm behind her head, wrapping her fingers in a thick juicy mat of ice plant and sea verbena, running her other hand along the silky hot dunes of Nick's spine, pulling him in. He seemed intoxicated by her, drinking her down like wine. It was glorious.

Dina told her parents she was sharing with a girlfriend while Nick roomed with another guy. She got a job checking groceries at the little market on Highway 1, where extra help was always needed to handle the summer people. While Dina packed milk and eggs into brown paper bags, Nick experimented with his circadian rhythms, going to sleep an hour later every other day, setting the alarm to wake himself an hour later too. Dina couldn't quite keep track of him: would he be wide awake when she came home from the grocery? Or would it be the middle of his personal night? By the time she had to go back to school, he'd completed his journey around the clock and was waking and sleeping at "normal" hours—he always drew those little quotation marks in the air when he said *normal*—but there was no denying that the eccentricity rooted in his character had sprouted, stretched and bloomed.

All summer long they'd had houseguests, mostly old friends of Nick's from New York. One was a homely girl—all nose, no chin—who behaved as if she were the most beautiful woman in the world. She liked to wrap herself in a white sheet as if it were a sarong, tucking a flower behind her ear. She'd sit on the couch slathering her smooth tan skin with coconut oil, so that little greasy spots appeared on every surface. The whole house smelled of coconut. Dina lay in bed craving Almond Joy bars. She bought herself one most every morning at the grocery store, taking advantage of her employee discount.

Another houseguest, bouncy, dizzy and talkative, had smeared her naked body with pigment to act in a Living Theatre production. Arielle dropped names that meant nothing to Dina, who could tell only that a certain inflection—a minuscule pause, a slight huskiness—signaled that a name had cultural weight. Prattling on about where she might go at summer's end, Arielle put on weight consuming the same food three times a day: bowl after bowl of muesli with heavy cream, baby food for adults.

Dina would come home to find Nick sitting with his visitors, shirtless, smoking dope, delighted to see her and offer her a hit. Dina wondered if he'd slept with the others while she worked, but she never asked. Everyone was so friendly. It seemed so bourgeois to worry. Besides, she trusted Nick. Like he always said, he believed in total honesty. And she believed in him. He couldn't help it if women were attracted to him; he was just that kind of guy.

❦   ❦   ❦

Nick drove to Berkeley to get Dina almost every weekend that fall. The beach in autumn was much as in summer, only quieter and cooler, more clouds and less company. But when she returned to Stinson during winter break, things began to change.

Nick introduced her to Gary, an "old friend from Berkeley" she'd somehow never seen before. Gary fit the profile later set in place by computer geeks—sunken-chested, skinny and pale, his thick glasses held together by adhesive tape wrapping a broken nosepiece. Gary was so shy he could hardly look at Dina. When he absolutely had to address her, he slid his eyes sideways to focus on her knee or her elbow, perhaps down to the floor at her feet. But Nick said he was a genius.

Gary was a Vietnam vet before that had become the name of a syndrome—this was '75, early days. He'd taken his chemistry degree to Southeast Asia, lived through his tour of duty, and come home with a bright idea for getting LSD into a more stable and far-out form than the sugar cubes or blotting paper most dealers used. The end product was a tiny translucent square, like a little chip of celluloid, with a miniature prism magically impressed in its center. When you held it up to the light, you saw a rainbow. They'd called their product "Pure

Light." Nick had shown surprising acuity as a marketer, packaging each gram—thousands of tiny hits—in a cunning little box he'd commissioned from a woodworker who lived near the beach. Every box was tied with a colorful length of Guatemalan weaving.

Soon everyone wanted Pure Light, and life was a little bit like minting money, like money for nothing. Nick bought the first of his dream houses, a short walk uphill from the beach, with its own walled patio where they could sunbathe nude and a kitchen where Dina could watch the tides as she stood at the sink. She and Nick agreed that the lab had to be off-site so Dina could have people to the house and, truth be told, so she could see a little less of an increasingly spectral and silent Gary (who, judging from his clothes, had done nothing at all with his share of the easy money, not even bought new jeans). Dina purchased a huge, clumsy used Steenbeck with cash Nick had given her—peeling it off a roll of hundreds like some mob boss in a gangster movie—and installed the bulky editing equipment in the spare room, churning out her documentaries like clockwork.

Nick's chosen profession didn't require much work. His days ran to sleeping late, walking along the beach or the ridgetop, reading the latest conspiracy theories, striking up odd friendships with the old farmers who still grew vegetables and raised cattle under the gnarled cypresses around Olema and Tomales Bay. The lab, all the technical stuff—that had been Gary's end. Nick's responsibilities involved late-night visits with guys in tight jeans and T-shirts with long nicotine-stained fingernails. They called each other "Man" at least once every sentence, otherwise saying very little that could be understood by outsiders to the code. They drank beer and smoked joints and exchanged inch-thick packets of cash for clever wooden parcels. They treated Dina with elaborate courtesy, like movie cowboys suppressing their natural exuberance in the presence of the boss's wife. It was a slightly sexy situation, all that male energy channeled into these tiny transactions. While these buyers were at the house, Dina stood behind Nick's chair stroking his neck. Or she sat at his feet, enjoying the electric feeling of his hands on her shoulders. She and Nick almost always made love after the visitors left. His ardor made her feel lucky and alive.

Decades later—after it had all flattened into memory—during an exchange of sisterly confidences, Dina's sister Deb—she'd been a kid during the counterculture Dina and her cohort had caught by the tail—had confessed how shocking and sordid she'd found the life Dina had described. "I mean, a drug dealer!" she'd said, "Duh! How stupid is that?"

Dina had explained it patiently. "There are good drugs and bad ones, and that has nothing to do with how the powers-that-be assign them to categories. It's about money and influence. Alcohol is the worst drug—the biggest health risks, the most crimes, the most accidents, the most fucked-up lives—but people who make and sell that drug are pillars of the community," she said scornfully. "Nicotine pushers are patrons of the arts. Caffeine is a national sacrament, and when you mix it with sugar—it's downright un-American not to swallow it. But smoke a little dope and see through that bullshit and you're evil personified." Deb hadn't really wanted to understand. The bottom line was, she didn't much like being out of control, and it made her nervous if anybody else got that way.

As far as Dina was concerned, the truly bad drugs made you feel puffed up with your own power. Coke, speed, crack—those were just a rum-and-cola and a cigarette, taken to the max. But the good drugs, the counterculture's drugs, had a spiritual aspect, dissolving the boundaries between people, enabling them to see connections that were hard to perceive with ordinary consciousness. People had been smoking dope, eating mushrooms—all that—since time immemorial. She had sometimes been afraid that Nick would be arrested, but never felt what he was doing was wrong.

In truth, Nick had been careful and ethical, a man of his word who was always keen to give value for money. If it had been legal, his business probably would have been one of those models of right livelihood that got profiled in the *Utne Reader*. His work gave her no reason to complain.

Indeed, life in those days was idyllic and sweet, except for certain moments Dina dreaded, and those had nothing at all to do with Nick's livelihood. It was when she screened her rough cuts for Nick that she was reminded they lived in two different mental universes.

It had happened a lot, but one particular time stood out, becoming in Dina's mind the archetype, the symbol of their misery. In 1980, when Reagan was elected, Dina knew some people who were part of a one-ring neighborhood circus in San Francisco that had been subsidized with public service employment funding. Reagan announced he would cut the funding program, and overnight, hundreds of artists who'd been paid to teach art to kids or paint community murals or perform in the parks were out of work. Dina had called up some people she knew, a shooter and a sound guy, and they'd schlepped all over the city, talking to clowns and painters and dancers who'd just lost the best gigs they'd ever had. The pay was low, they told the camera, but the satisfaction was unbeatable, getting to do their work for people who had never seen any benefit from the many millions of tax dollars spent on opera houses with red velvet drapes and golden chandeliers.

Dina had been so excited by the footage, she'd stayed up till sunrise night after night to cut it together, jumping out of bed after a few hours' sleep to start again. The story reached a sort of crescendo with a performance by the jazz combo that accompanied the circus, an original tune they'd written for the soundtrack, *Ronnie Ray-gun's Blues*. The final segment intercut footage of all the artists they'd interviewed, driving the point home: *Look what's already being lost.*

When the film ended and Dina turned on the lights, Nick had been standing by his chair with one arm in a raised fist and his head bowed, like Tommie Smith and John Carlos in their black power protest at the 1968 Olympics. She felt as if he'd punched her in the stomach.

Later, when he couldn't stand her moping around the house, they talked about it. Nick was earnest, uncommonly serious, trying to explain. "How are people going to get to see this thing?" he asked.

"The usual ways. Maybe public TV. Maybe one of the video collectives will distribute it. There'll be screenings around the city, I'm sure the artists will want to use it."

"In other words, the people who see it will already agree with it. So is that your intention, to reinforce what they already know?"

"I don't think they do know it," Dina insisted. "I think if people had the real information—if they understood how Reagan's policies are already affecting ordinary people in the neighborhoods, they'd respond."

"Write their Congressman? Give money to the fund for starving artists?" Nick asked. "Respond how?"

"All of that," said Dina, "and more. Keep Reagan from getting his way."

"Look, Dina." Nick sighed with exasperation, tucking his hair behind his ears. Why couldn't she see what was obvious? "These people are idiots. Either by voting for him or doing nothing to stop him, they elected Reagan. You believe that knowing some artists lost their jobs is going to make them rise up? Most people could care less. You've made a rousing call to arms here. I just don't think anybody is listening."

❦   ❦   ❦

Sometimes, looking back, Dina wondered how they had kept it together all those years. When she felt like being hard on herself, she wondered if staying with Nick hadn't been the real sellout: for a house at the beach and the price of editing equipment, she'd been willing to overlook the fact that her partner had no respect for her work. But that wasn't really true, or at least not the whole truth. She'd loved Nick and she'd had Nick's love in return, even though it had come packaged with his bone-deep cynicism.

She and Nick had made a life together, with all that entailed: knowing each other's little habits and quirks and pleasures, sleeping in each other's arms, having heard the other's childhood anecdotes once or twice too often (but forbearing to say so), wiring around the sore spots. Twenty years is a long time— an investment if you live happily ever after, a waste if you leave it all behind. Thrifty Dina tried to hang in there with Nick, but in the end, she had to let it go. She couldn't hitch her life to someone who felt the need to shit on any manifestation of idealism, or even hope.

At a certain point, without really deciding to, she began increasing the distance between the two of them. Gradually, Nick's opinions ceased to shape her life. In between her own film productions, she'd started to take commissions. They'd been promotional films for worthy organizations, that sort of thing. It made her feel good to be bringing in her own money. She found she liked helping other people tell their stories. Her satisfied clients introduced her to others who could use help, and after a few years, a sideline in promotional films had elided into ads for selected candidates and issue campaigns.

Nick and Gary continued to satisfy their clients too. LSD had peaked, but the Eighties were a boom time for designer drugs, especially MDMA, which was later called Ecstasy. Those two were on the job with their own brand, "Upward," which reduced the jaw-clenching tension usually associated with the drug. Each tab had a little arrow impressed on one side. No handmade wooden boxes, but still, a quality product and a big moneymaker. By the '90s, each of them had enough money in real estate, stashes of cash, and offshore accounts to last two lifetimes.

Sometimes the guys wondered aloud why they kept making money, why they didn't give it up. Nick made sketchy plans for a big retirement when he turned thirty-five, then forty: he might buy a big piece of land in Alaska, or even an island somewhere warm. But that was all idle dreaming. Gary still lived in his little shack, still wore his ancient plaid shirts; and beyond dreaming about the farther reaches of real estate, Nick couldn't really make himself want anything he hadn't already bought. When Dina asked why they didn't just stop then, Nick merely shrugged and said, "It's what I do."

Sometimes she loved coming back to the house in Stinson Beach after a long day of setting up shots and conducting interviews. When you knew the road well enough, driving along Highway 1 from Mill Valley became a kind of dance, arms sweeping first left, then right, as the road threaded through the mountains. At certain turns, a long fringe of eucalyptus brushed the car, releasing its pungent fragrance. Then the countryside opened into green hills and steep valleys. In spring, she kept watch for the earliest golden poppies, the surprising red of paintbrush, the purple spikes of lupine. If she got home before sunset, the first sight of the Pacific always stopped her breath, shards of crystal caught in a net of bluest green.

If Nick was in a good mood, he'd welcome her home with a glass of wine and a joint. They'd sit and watch the spectacle, always hoping to see the green flash as the sun sank on the horizon. In their personal system of omens, that signaled a good night to come. They'd cook dinner, dance a little to the stereo, make love on the patio. There was something between them that always burned, needing the merest spark to set it off.

Other times she found Nick curled in a chair, his handsome face like a fist. He'd have spent the day listening to NPR or Pacifica, storing up contempt. Instead of a hello, he'd greet her with the latest outrage from a corrupt order in the final stages of disintegration. She resisted the temptation to point out that for a moribund system, it retained considerable power to inflame Nick. *That elitist idiot Bush got tired of paying Noriega off, so now we were invading Panama—Panama!* Each successive outrage pushed him further from the larger society. *That spineless wuss Bill Clinton blew off Lani Guinier at the first sign of opposition!*

He had reason to be angry. It was just that his anger immobilized and isolated him. Nick seldom talked to anyone but his local cronies and business associates. He didn't answer the phone because there were too many people he didn't want to speak to. After awhile—no visits, no calls, not even a hello—Dina's parents stopped asking after him and started suggesting that she might want to meet So-and-so's nephew, who just happened to be in town.

Nick hardly left the beach. It was impossible for Dina to coax him into the city for one of her screenings. He hadn't visited his own parents since 1990. He hadn't even gone East for his father's funeral in '93. When Dina asked him about it, all Nick said was that his father wouldn't know whether he was there or not. Funerals were supposed to be for the living, and he couldn't imagine his presence lending the living any comfort. Dina hadn't been able to argue that point with even a smidgen of conviction.

By the time Hal Crayton was elected governor in 1994, Dina had been doing his TV spots straight through two terms in the State Senate as a crusader for public accountability. She liked the man, and although he wasn't pure by the standards Nick liked to declaim—you had to kiss a lot of butts to raise enough money to run for the California State Senate—she felt his commitments were genuine, that he had a soul. In some vague boy scout gee-whiz way, he reminded her of her father. Before she accepted the job, they'd gotten drunk together and confided their deepest dreams. Hal (he was still Hal in those days, not yet Governor Crayton) had gotten all misty-eyed about democracy in a way Dina didn't think could be faked. She thought of Nick's ivory armchair, thought she had better get her hands dirty if she didn't want to wind up there, lonely in the certainty of her critique.

She packed her stuff and left for Sacramento. The first night away, she missed Nick in every cell of her body, aching for him as she hadn't in years. Fighting shame, she picked up the phone. "Nick, it's me."

"Long time no see," he said, sounding sardonic and stoned.

Dina pushed ahead, her heart booming. "I'm here in my new place, and everything feels kind of empty and incomplete. You could drive up here. I'd inaugurate the kitchen, cook you some dinner. Just help me over this hump. What do you say, Nick?"

He just laughed into the mouthpiece and put the phone down.

CHAPTER 3

❀

Nick found it a little surreal to fall into scheming together after so many years of silence, but somehow it also felt right. It was some kind of connection, anyway. Once he understood that Dina really meant what she was saying—Gandhi and all—he did his best to respond in kind.

"So you're asking me if this can be done, right?"

"Right. I figured if anybody would know…" Dina trailed off, feeling lame.

Nick tried to sound reassuring. "Well, I do keep up, if I say so myself. Or rather, Gary keeps up, and we keep in touch. Some of what they're doing these days with designer drugs, it's amazing."

"That's what I was hoping," Dina said. "But now that I'm here, it seems crazy to just jump into this conversation with you. I mean, there's been a lot of water—and other stuff—under the bridge since we last sat down together." She rubbed her forehead, raked her fingers through her curls. "Can we even trust each other?"

"I don't think trust was our issue," Nick said, his expression pained. "You didn't lie to me or betray me. You were a woman of your word."

"You kept your word too," Dina allowed, thinking it over. "It had more to do with our values, what we wanted from life."

Oh yes, said Nick's inner voice, *tell her you've had a values transplant. I'm sure that'll win her over.* Nick ignored it. "So let's not jump into anything," he told Dina. "I say we take a crack at this, but in a completely provisional way, okay?"

"What do you mean?"

"Let's talk about how it *might* work, but not commit to doing anything unless both of us are absolutely sure. Sort of an as-if approach."

Dina thought it over, letting her gaze float along the polished wood surfaces. "There's this voice in my head saying *oh-oh*," she told him.

Nick shook his head. "I know what you mean." *More than you might think.* "Let's both take pieces of paper and write down what we fear, what might go wrong—the reasons not to try to do this together. We don't have to show our notes to each other, just put them in our pockets. Then if this thing seems real, we can pull out our lists before we decide whether to go ahead. If fears trump hopes, we'll blow it off, no harm done. What d'you say?"

Try as she might, Dina couldn't find anything wrong with this suggestion. Nick took a yellow legal pad from a drawer and handed her the top sheet. She made her list quickly, as if taking dictation. It was all the right there on the top of her mind:

> I'll think things are okay and all the time, he'll be judging me
> Once burned, twice shy
> Why go backwards?
> It took a long time to get away the first time
> I'll fall for him again and he'll hurt me

Nick's list, though shorter, took more time to produce:

> SHE WON'T BE INTERESTED IN ME, JUST THIS SCHEME
> I'LL WIND UP ALONE AGAIN, FEELING IT MORE
> I'LL DISAPPOINT HER SOMEHOW

When Nick looked up, Dina was watching him. He felt himself flush, turned it into a joke. "Hard work dredging up the fears, hmm?"

Dina smiled.

Nick tapped his list. "It's not going to be easy to ignore these."

"You're telling me?"

Nick folded his sheet in quarters and dropped it into his pocket. Dina stuck hers in her purse.

"Okay," said Nick. "I have an idea. Let's pretend we're doing an RFP for this new drug."

"'RFP'?" Dina was taken aback. "Do you have some secret hobby as a bureaucrat or something?"

Nick bristled. *She thinks you're a fool, man,* said his inner voice. *That's the top of her list, no doubt: "How can I get mixed up with this fool again?"* "No," Nick told Dina, "I've been in suspended animation since the last time you saw me. Haven't learned a thing."

Dina blushed.

Nick decided to be big about it. Besides, he didn't think he had much to gain by enumerating the string of obsessions that had kept him informed and distracted the last few years: Icelandic sagas, investigating Costa Rican real estate, learning all he could about Egyptian funerary portraits, about jazz pianists, about organic vegetable gardening.

"I've been involved in some habitat restoration work here on the mountain," he told Dina, "people getting together to clean up streams and do a little reforestation. It's all pretty much regulated, so I know a whole bunch of initials now: EIR, RFP—there's no end to them."

"I'm sorry, Nick. I'm an idiot. Why should I think your life has stood still any more than mine?"

"Indeed." He liked that wide-eyed look of contrition, tugging less at his heart than somewhere a little lower down. "Brown-Eyed Girl" was still his favorite Van Morrison song. *But this isn't about that, remember?* He picked up the pad and began to make notes. "So you want it to wake people up, right? Like speed or coke?"

"No, no. Not like staying up all night gritting your teeth. Like coming into awareness, you know?"

"Okay," said Nick, making a note. "Heightened awareness. Like marijuana?"

"I guess so." Dina thought about it. "But not so the awareness leads to giggles. This is serious."

"Like serious pot."

"This is the longest I've ever spent with you that we didn't get stoned, speaking of serious pot."

He squinted at her. "You still do that?"

"Do you?"

"Ah, the caution of the non-hobbyist bureaucrat." Nick bit his tongue, not liking the way Dina's smile closed down at his remark. "Yes, I still do it," he told her, "but generally not first thing in the morning, and generally not to work." He laughed, shaking his head. "And if you'd told me twenty years ago that I would someday utter that sentence, I would have laughed in your face."

"Twenty years ago we were still in Stinson Beach, and ideas like 'first thing in the morning' and 'work' didn't have much meaning." Dina stared out the window, imagining the ocean in place of a sea of grass, remembering the dunes, her fingers gripping the succulent vines. *But this isn't about that,* she told herself. *Right?*

"Do you ever miss it?" Beginning to know his own heart, Nick hoped he also knew what Dina's answer would be.

"Yeah," she sighed, after a long pause, giving in to whatever this was. "I do. But then I get confused. What am I missing? Something about the life we led? Or just being young and dumb and hopeful?"

"Okay," said Nick, briskly returning to business. He wasn't ready to go *there* just yet. "Heightened awareness, serious pot, what else?"

"I want people to be able to see through things," said Dina, suddenly solemn.

"Like Superman?" When she didn't respond, Nick dropped the joke. "Like acid? When you suddenly see something for what it is?"

"Not exactly. Acid seems too risky. That kind of seeing through things can create a false consciousness too. God!" Dina smiled, shaking her head at the images floating there. "I remember dropping acid in that first house on the beach and having to go outside because the colors on all those posters started looking very squirmy and artificial and malevolent, and I really needed to see green—blue sky, green grass, true colors."

Dina sat up straighter, recalled to urgency. "Nick, you have to promise me something."

He raised his eyebrows.

"If this comes together, there cannot be any bad trips. This cannot be something that makes people think they can fly off a roof or even makes them want to barf every time they look at their wall posters. If this can't be clean—if it risks doing *any* type of harm—it can't happen." She stared straight into his eyes. "Promise me."

"I can't promise we'll be able to make the totally risk-free drug, Dina. And remember, we haven't even decided to try yet."

She nodded, looking deflated.

"But you have my pledge I won't settle for anything less. If we can't make it right, we won't make it, period." Nick had his doubts about this pledge—even aspirin wasn't risk-free—but it was clear that unless he offered it, his new partnership with Dina wasn't going any further, and by now he wanted it to, no question.

"I believe you, Nick." *After all this time*, she thought, *I still believe you.*

It took all morning to build their criteria:

Heightened awareness (serious pot)
Seeing through things (but not seeing everything as false)
No harmful effects, no risks
Reality check—seeing past the false fronts and cover stories
Sharp thinking, no impairment of logical thought
Ego-bridging, not ego-reinforcing

> Pleasurable, but not euphoric or intoxicating
> No impairment of communication or physical functioning, able
> to go about life
> No stimulation of abstract feelings (e.g., sudden raging lust,
> hunger, fear)—feelings should fit situation

"I just have one more question," said Nick. "What do we call it? I wish we hadn't used 'Pure Light' already. Purity?"

"Sounds too much like virginity," said Dina. "Something less goody-goody."

"Lucidity?"

"That's not bad, but would people call it 'Lucy'? And if they did, would that make it seem goofy?"

Nick pulled out his pen again. "Maybe we need to make a list about the name too, get clear what image we want to project."

"Clear!" Dina was out of her seat. "That's it: Clarity. And you know what they'll call it, if my media skills are worth their salt? C! Get it? 'Take C to see clearly.'"

Then she sat down again, suddenly looking discouraged. "Well, that all sounds great, but it's just words on paper. Be honest with me, Nick. Is this just a silly dream? Or is it really possible?"

Nick hesitated. "Well, I don't want to get your hopes up," he said, "but this isn't all that far-fetched based on some of the stuff Gary's been working on for quite awhile now. You know Gary, he'd just keep on tinkering and tweaking forever. The search interests him more than the result, you know?"

"To travel hopefully is a better thing than to arrive," said Dina with a smile.

"Robert Louis Stevenson," said Nick, pointing to his head. "Still got that quotations database my father installed. What I mean is Gary doesn't have any big need to get back into circulation. The opposite. He's up in Alaska, you know."

"Really? Your old dream."

"Yeah, but he did it. He even hooked up with a woman, if you can believe that—one who's more shy than he is!"

Dina shook her head, struggling to imagine.

"But from what he's told me, I get the feeling his new design is basically operational, and not that much of a stretch from our RFP here. But I have to run all this by him and see if he's willing to tweak some more and share the results. For old times' sake."

"For old times' sake," said Dina, sipping her cold tea, daring to hope against hope.

Dina went straight back to her office in the capitol, masking both her excitement and her anxiety with work. The biggest thing on her desk was a standing file crammed with at least fifty folders, each crying out for immediate attention. Her colleague Gabe joked that she should make a huge sign marked "urgent" and just paste it over the whole kit and caboodle. Well, it was true; in various ways all of them were urgent. Whether or not Clarity became real, she wasn't going to be working at the governor's office much longer, but while she was still here, she would do her best to take care of business.

Dina didn't go in for homey office décor—no family pictures or miniature stuffed animals for her, no African violet in a cute ceramic pot. Most of her wall space was a messy collage of flyers, clippings, charts and timelines. But a framed sampler held pride of place on the wall over her desk, a cross-stitched quote from Voltaire: "The perfect is the enemy of the good." One day a French visitor had corrected it. What Voltaire had actually said was *"Le mieux est l'ennemi du bien."* The best is the enemy of the good. But that seemed a little less inspiring, so she went right on misquoting.

So while Nick consulted Gary, Dina poured her heart and soul into a doomed campaign to balance Native American fishing rights with commercial fishing interests. She wasn't supposed to be doing this one either—she'd have to work late to catch up with the plan for her next press conference—but a friend had begged so hard she couldn't say no. It was shaping up as one of those lose-lose propositions: whichever way the ultimate plan went, somebody was going to be very unhappy. Environmentalists wouldn't be satisfied until most salmon fishing stopped. The men who operated the dwindling fleet of fishing boats off the north coast saw their livelihoods disappearing with every concession. The Native Americans had already been so fucked over, even a total victory on a specific issue like this failed to register much approval from that quarter. So there was no big win to be had. Yet Dina was able—as always—to keep her nose to the grindstone with frequent reminders that, had the Republicans been in the statehouse, the environmentalists and Indians wouldn't have gotten anything at all.

❧　　　　❧　　　　❧

A week after Dina's visit to Nick, he phoned her, using their oblique style of communication from the old days, as if the phone lines were being monitored by sinister authorities.

"I spoke to that guy I mentioned," Nick told her.

"Uh-huh." Dina was unsure what she wanted to hear. Maybe it would be better to drop the whole thing.

"I think we should meet," said Nick. He suggested a coffee shop in Vallejo, about midway between Healdsburg and Sacramento, and Dina consented.

That stretch of highway is about as straight and boring as any in California. Usually, Dina had to crank down all the windows and turn up the radio to avoid falling asleep as she passed mile after mile of strip developments and flat, open fields. This time, she had her anxiety and ambivalence to keep her company. Still, the drive seemed endless, and she inhaled huge draughts of sweet, dusty valley air to keep herself focused on the road.

Nick's instructions led her to a typical truck stop with a herd of semis in the parking lot and inside, a flock of orange leatherette booths filled with big men in plaid shirts with the sleeves rolled up, wearing caps with logos on them. Scanning for Nick, she ignored several suggestive invitations from tables of beefy strangers. When a waitress wearing an orange apron with her name embroidered above the pocket presented a menu, Dina almost refused, doubting she'd found the right place. Then she felt a hand on her shoulder and turned around.

"I think you'll like the chicken-fried steak," said Nick, grinning.

A face as familiar as home: blue eyes, crooked smile, the outlines of a known world. A feeling of relief swept through Dina's body. Her arms began to lift toward an embrace, and in an instant, relief turned to alarm. *What was this? Talk about leaping before you look—this is not the plan.* To cover herself, Dina pointed to the menu in her upraised hand. "It says here the specialty is fried *pies*, not steak."

"Can I get that with a side of fries?"

"Or maybe just cut to the chase and mainline some cooking grease." The air was pungent with it—hot fat, charred meat, coffee grounds.

When they were ensconced in squeaky orange leatherette and supplied with thick white mugs of bad coffee, Nick began his report. "So, like I said, I talked to that guy."

Dina raised her eyebrows, waiting.

"He says he can do it, Dina. He says it's basically what he was working on anyway—that there's some kind of synchronicity about these things, like the Wright Brothers and Gabriel Voisin working on aviation at the same time, or the way they give scientific prizes to teams who've been working on the same discovery, but not together."

"I'm amazed," said Dina. "I was braced for disappointment. I wondered if this could be real, and now you're telling me it is. And not just in Gary's mind, right? He's tested it, it's safe, all that? You're absolutely certain?"

"Dina, think about it. You know Gary. He's a belt-and-suspenders guy, right? That hasn't changed, unless he's become more cautious." Nick leaned in close to whisper in her ear. "He had me go out and call him at some new number from a safe phone, Dina. And then he still talked like the fucking CIA. He says it's completely doable, and the process is simple and cheap, much easier than the things he used to do."

Dina felt excitement rise from the pit of her stomach. And then she felt anxiety push it down. "Oh, God," she said.

"Oh, God how great or oh, God how…what?"

"Both. Are we going to do this? I've got somebody looking over my shoulder saying '*Watch out!*'"

"Who is it?" Nick knew the speaker who hovered near his own shoulder, the one that said he was good for nothing, a waste of food and water. But he didn't think Dina set aside real estate in her mental landscape for that voice.

"I don't know, Nick," she said, shaking her head. "Either it's my guardian angel who's just looking after my best interests, or it's the part of me that's too tired to take a risk. Take your pick."

Nick pulled a folded yellow sheet from his pocket. "Have you got yours?"

Dina fished in her purse and came up with her list of reservations, somewhat stained and crumpled. She smoothed it out on the orange formica table.

"Okay," said Nick. "Let's read them over and think really hard. If either of us wants to give it a pass, just stand up and say goodbye, and that will be that, no hard feelings."

The waitress refilled their cups as they read. When she asked if they wanted to eat anything, Nick asked her to come back in five minutes.

It was like a staring contest without the staring. By the time the waitress came back, neither Nick nor Dina had moved. Nick ordered a steak sandwich and Dina a piece of apricot pie, first ascertaining that it was baked, not fried.

"We need some working agreements, though. I'm not going into this without a seat belt," said Dina.

"Okay," said Nick, suppressing any outward sign of his glee. "Like what?"

"Like we have to try it first, obviously, and if we have any doubts after that, we bail."

"Understood." Nick dropped his fist onto the table like a gavel.

"Total security, no exposure."

"Grant me some knowledge of how to do that," he said. "I've had decades of practice."

Dina nodded. "And either one of us can call a halt if we feel we've made a mistake or it just isn't working—or whatever."

"Done," said Nick, smiling at the waitress who was airlifting their plates from the string of orders balanced along the length of her arm.

Trembling with excitement and wondering if she'd done the right thing, Dina drove home without noticing the moonlit grass, its liquid silver shimmer as the wind moved across its surface, the night sky filled with stars. Exhausted, she fell into bed and immediately into sleep, five dreamless hours before the sound of her early-bird alarm.

❦   ❦   ❦

Six weeks to the day after she had visited Nick to put the proposition of the new drug, Dina was back at his place for a test drive. In between, they spent a lot of time on the phone.

"Those photos you wanted are almost ready," Nick said in his penultimate call. "We just need to get the print a little sharper, there's still some distortion."

"Take your time," Dina replied. "We really can't have any distortion at all. It has to be crystal-clear."

When Nick called to set up that day's meeting, all he said was, "Your photos are ready."

During the entire drive from Sacramento, Dina was hugely nervous, butterflies, shakes, the whole nine yards. Now, as Nick explained what Gary had told him to expect, Dina kept losing the thread of the conversation, tuning instead into her own inner broadcast: was she here because of Nick, and Clarity just a cover? Or was she torturing herself with Nick in the interests of Clarity?

"No jaw-clenching neck pain thing," Nick was saying. "No nausea or any other strong physical sensation."

"Good," mumbled Dina, recalling one trip where all she could do was rub the back of her stiff neck while watching the wallpaper designs endlessly transform.

"…just a strong sense of presence. You should feel focused in the here and now, aware of everything that's going on, including your own mental processes…"

Dina forbore to say that her own here-and-now mental processes resembled a rat in a maze. She hoped she didn't have to stay trapped there all day. She careened from unease over the drug to trepidation about spending the day alone with Nick, to excitement about both—then back again.

"So be sure to drink plenty of liquid, because we want to keep it moving through your system, get a good idea of how long it lasts."

Dina chugged another glass of water. Her mother used to say if she drank too much, her eyeballs would float. "I'm ready," she told Nick.

He handed her a small white tablet, perfectly round and blank. "Sorry," he said, "no time yet for logos or whatever. This is the prototype." He popped one into his own mouth and drank, watching as Dina did likewise. Then they moved to the porch swing to wait.

At first, it was a déjà vu of every trip they'd taken. Looking at the clock. Asking "do you feel anything yet?" Saying "I think I feel something. My eyes feel sort of big." Or, "I have sort of a buzzy feeling in my legs." After about an hour, they looked at one another and laughed.

"Hello," said Nick, gazing into Dina's big brown eyes.

"Hello," said Dina, smiling back. Her vision clicked sideways, like a slide coming into focus, and suddenly she was aware of seeing Nick as if for the first time. A tender expression, with flashes of something that looked like anxiety. The gray at his temples. The creases at the corners of his eyes that somehow set off the blue, deep and cool between the pale lashes. The dimples her mother had admired were now lines from nose to chin. When Dina stared hard, she could make out the young Nick just behind this face. With effort, she could toggle back and forth between the two Nicks. He was still there, all his grace and pride and wariness, the same yet not the same.

"I feel like I can really see you," Nick told her, "for the first time in years. Your mouth," he reached out to touch it, "seems even softer now, your eyes…"

"This is what we've made of ourselves," Dina said, sweeping her gaze over their faces and bodies. She felt suffused with tenderness. It reminded her of the time a workshop leader asked participants to view themselves through God's eyes. All her misdeeds and imperfections had suddenly seemed no more than the sweet foibles of a beloved child. "We started out to be these innocent little sprouts with these ordinarily fucked-up families," she told Nick. "You wanted to run away from the world, and I wanted to run toward it, and here we are a few decades later, a little wrinkled and gray, meeting halfway."

Nick's eyes filled with tears, but he said nothing. He'd been running a long time, mostly in his mind: Iceland, ancient Egypt. It had never felt far enough. Now, all at once, it seemed so clear: Dina had been the thing that had made his life, that made him real. When he lost her—to his own stubbornness, his stupid determination not to care—he lost himself, and he could run forever without finding anything. A teardrop fell along his nose, sliding into the furrow beside his mouth. *Right*, said his inner voice. *Bawling. That'll get her for sure.*

Dina didn't think she'd ever seen Nick cry. She followed the tear's progress along the groove bracketing his mouth. His parentheses, she'd always called them, enclosing the words left unsaid. She thought of the millions of words she'd missed these many years apart, how she could never get them back. As soon as the thought came to consciousness, she felt her body stiffen, putting up a wall of flesh. Normally, her defenses would have kicked in, automatic and unconscious, but under the influence of Clarity, she was aware of every muscle fiber contracting. How much had her life—her seemingly independent life—been shaped by pushing away from Nick, whose tears moved her so deeply?

Nick sensed his chance. His inner voice protested, but he paid it no mind. "I regret the running, Dina. I really do." He shook his head. "When I think about it, I wish the world hadn't let me get away with running. If money hadn't come so easily. If you hadn't been there so soon, before I could really understand what you meant to me. If my parents had given a shit."

Nick looked into Dina's eyes, heedless of his own spilling over. "No, no. Forget all that bullshit. If I'd had the guts." *You got that right*, hissed the voice.

Dina reached out to wipe away Nick's tears. It was the first time she'd touched him since they'd reconnected. "It was what it was," she said. "I have regrets too. But we're not dead yet. We could make a *tikkun*. We can do *t'shuvah*."

"A what?"

"It's Hebrew." She took a deep breath, knowing an explanation was in order. "Being Jewish means much more to me than when we lived together. When I was young, it was just a way of saying I was different. The reason we didn't have Christmas. The reason why I got teased or chased by some Catholic kids in the neighborhood. But that was all. Then I started doing a little studying as part of my film project..." Dina left space for Nick's deprecating laugh, but it didn't come.

Instead he asked a question. "So you believe in God now? That there's somebody watching over us? You have faith?"

Dina could see that Nick still found this impossible to conceive. What's more, she understood why. He'd been trained from childhood in the intellectual style that makes logic its god. If she'd had these insights in the old days, she would have been afraid to tell him, to risk his scorn. "It's not so much about what I believe," she explained, "it's what I stopped believing—in the human arrogance that wants to reduce everything to the physical world so it can be controlled. I doubt there's a big-daddy God in the sky keeping a list of who's naughty and nice. But I think the world is more than chemicals and electrical charges. I don't *know* anything, except that there's a mystery at the center of our existence, a power in the universe beyond our control. One day I asked myself how my life would be different if I believed it was possible to align myself with that power."

Nick felt himself on shaky ground. Part of him said she sounded like a Moonie, like someone trying to push her religious trip. The other part didn't believe Dina could surrender her brain to some cult, and didn't want to risk making her think he did. "And now you know how to do that?" he asked. "And it's, like, Jewish? That specific religion, rather than spirituality in general?"

"No," Dina laughed, "I can't say I know how for certain. I mean, I haven't gotten the secret password to a higher power or anything. But I was so sad after the first year or two in Sacramento. I lost the point of living. It felt like a lot of work for no discernible difference. I had this huge passion to heal the world, but as far as I could see, I hadn't made any progress at all. In fact, it felt like I'd lost ground. And then this idea came to me out of the blue. What if I looked at my life so far not as a failure but as a form of preparation for a particular task to come, *my* task?

"I have this friend Nancy—she teaches at Sac State—and I told her about it. She gave me this book that said that each person is prepared for a unique role in life, the way each letter of Torah is unique, and omitting it changes the meaning of the whole. I realized there were all these reasons for me to be a Jew, not just a vaguely 'spiritual person.'" She laughed. "I mean, how can I turn my back on a religion that treats disputation as a form of worship? Is that part of my DNA or what?"

Nick laughed too, acknowledging the obvious.

"I love the way Judaism is a religion in time instead of space, you know?"

"Not really. What do you mean?" This made him nervous. Was she proselytizing?

"Like we don't have cathedrals—Heschel said that Shabbat is our cathedral. The whole year has a cycle of holidays, each with its own purpose and intention, so you go through the year focusing in turn on various aspects of your development: are you living up to your intentions? Are your actions helping to repair the world? I'm not interested in submitting myself to some type of religious authority—I haven't become a disciple or something like that. But I'm Jewish in my own way because it fits me. That's all." She laughed. "And just in case you're worried, I'm not recruiting."

Nick felt a little sheepish, but he thought he understood her. "And has it made a difference in your life?"

"Not every minute," admitted Dina. "But a lot of the time, yes. I see now that my ideas about healing the world aren't just my individual neurotic symptoms. They have a lineage. I decided to try to live as if my passions have a purpose, to shine a light on my special task, as if my history had truly been preparation. As if I could bring my own life into alignment with a higher healing intention. Sometimes I can't get there. But you know what they say? 'Fake it till you make it.'"

"Is that Torah?" Nick asked, smiling despite himself.

"Not word for word." Dina could see he wasn't too comfortable with all this. She tried to bring it down to earth. "But how would your life be different if you lived as if it were true?"

Nick sighed, rolling his eyes. Maybe she had a point. "Let me count the ways."

"This one rabbi I know talks about 'spiritual technologies,' and that's what I try to use to help myself stay awake. Like those words I used. A *tikkun* is a repair. In the sense I was using, it has to do with fixing the past, the idea that you can do something now that corrects an earlier misstep. *T'shuvah* is usually translated as repentance, but literally it means turning, reorientation. While the rest of the world thinks no one can ever change—if they mess up, you just have to lock them up forever—*t'shuvah* says it's never too late, you're never too far away to perform the small turn that reorients your life."

Nick had that preoccupied look, as if he were having a silent debate with himself.

Dina filled her lungs with air and forced herself to say what she couldn't stop thinking. "What I was wondering, Nick, is if we could do this thing with Clarity, if we could help to wake people up, that might also heal whatever regrets we have about parts of our own lives, about making them less than they could have been."

After that, they talked an endless stream of words about everything that had remained unspoken between them for so many years. All the times Dina had a little triumph or disappointment at work and found herself suppressing the impulse to tell Nick about it; all the strange things Nick had learned and the troubling habit of mind that set him to imagine sharing them with Dina, remembering only later that Dina was no longer in his life. Each association led to another and another, a tapestry of speech spun from years of silence.

"I've missed you," Nick told her at last, feeling as if he were jumping off a cliff.

As Dina felt the same words begin to take shape in her own mouth, the other side of the coin turned up. Her lips stayed shut, bending into a tense smile. Nick could have picked up a phone sometime in the last seven years. He could have avoided driving her away in the first place. She sighed. "I don't know how to talk about this, Nick. You knew where I was, but there must have been some reason you didn't try to get in touch. So how much did you miss me, really? And how much of me are you seeing now? Enough to know whether it's me you miss? Or just a memory?"

"More than enough!" he insisted. "The *tikkun* I want to make is between you and me, Dina. I especially want to fix how I treated you towards the end."

"Why?" Dina cut Nick off before he could answer the wrong question. "No, I'm not asking why you want to fix it. I mean why did it happen in the first place? I thought you hated my work. I thought you saw me as a sap who cared about things that weren't worth it. Was that it?"

"No, no." Nick rubbed his eyes. "But, shit, I can see how you'd think that. Remember film school? Everybody thought my half-baked little projects were so cool. I kept it to myself, but deep down inside, I wanted to be a great director—Antonioni or Godard or maybe Orson Welles. And every time I thought about it, I heard that voice saying, 'Second-rate Godard. Second-rate Antonioni.' My fucking father, I let him get in my head and I never chased him out. I was so sure of what he would say, and so sure he was probably right, I couldn't make myself risk it. Instead, I stumbled onto something that was easy and fat and nobody in the world could say if I was doing it right or not. You know, there weren't any generally accepted professional standards for LSD distribution—no critics, no fathers. I was the invisible man, and I thought that made me free." Nick scrubbed his hair off his forehead and took a breath.

"And then you were out there, Dina, just doing it. You didn't need to beat yourself over the head with the geniuses of cinema. You had stories to tell, and you got them out. And you did it well, with craft and conviction that showed my whole grandiose fantasy for what it was, a bunch of excuses that kept me from really getting down to it. Your enthusiasm embarrassed me. It was uncool in a way that reflected on me. I hated myself every time I did it, but it was like I didn't have any choice: I had to put you down or call my own trip into question, and I wasn't ready to do that." Nick rubbed his forehead. *What an asshole you were*, said the inner voice. "What an asshole I was," said Nick.

"Are you ready to look at those questions now?" asked Dina. But then she wasn't entirely sure she wanted to hear the answer, so she hurried to fill up the silence. "You know, I talk to your picture quite a lot. It sits near my computer. When I'm feeling bitter, late at night, I like to say I wasted my youth on you." Dina laughed at the turn of phrase. "I can see somebody like Susan Hayward saying that, looking up from her glass and just spitting it at Clark Gable. But the truth is, in a way, you saved me, Nick."

He looked surprised.

"Before I met you, I was a good girl. I put a lot of energy into impersonating the all-American girl, the good-daughter counterpart to Bernie's *Father Knows Best* act. He and Charlotte were so sure I'd grow out of the filmmaker thing, and I halfway thought they were right. That I'd go along and one day turn into my mother, without really understanding how it had happened. I was so clueless, I sometimes wonder how anyone could be that young and out of it."

Dina gazed into the distance of memory. "You know, in junior high, I had a teacher who gave us the assignment of writing an essay on our philosophy of life. I really struggled over that thing. I wasn't really sure what a philosophy of life was, but it seemed really important, like having this key that made every-thing fit together. When I first met you, I thought, here's a guy who has a phi-losophy of life!"

They both laughed, but Nick's laughter was incredulous.

"No, I'm not kidding. You did! When I finally took philosophy, I even found out what it was—skepticism. I was so impressed. I was so thrilled that you were interested in me, this cool, talented, adventurous guy with an actual philoso-phy. All I really wanted was your approval.

"My professor said that skepticism was about remaining open to the possi-bility of truth while continuing to search for it. Remember that mescaline trip we took out at the beach? The one where I saw you floating off the ground on a long, golden cord, almost like a kite? I thought you were above ordinary things, that there was something high and fine about you, like you were some type of lookout, like you had chosen an observation post.

"But I was very young in those days, and I didn't see the fear behind the way you chose to keep your distance. I should have, because after Pure Light, your skepticism took a dark turn. It seemed to me you came to the conclusion that there was no truth, at least none that could be discovered, understood, commu-nicated. And I remember it so vividly, realizing that I didn't see things that way. The big surprise was recognizing that I had my own take on the world and it was independent of yours, that I didn't want to just take your trip for the rest of my life. I wasn't a good girl anymore—loose living and chemicals had cured me of that—and what I really wanted was to be fully myself, to be good at inhabit-ing my own life. And that's what took me away from you and me, from us.

"And the thing is, Nick, if you hadn't kept running from life, I don't think I would have seen that my path didn't go that way. I could have been like my mother, just latching onto someone else's life and riding it out. I doubt I ever would have been forced back onto my own inner resources, to find my own direction. So what you feel regret about—well, yeah, it wasn't much fun for me at the time. It was agony to have you laugh at my ideals and treat my work like shit. I'd like to go on excoriating you for stealing my youth; it gives me such a righteous buzz." Dina laughed, shaking her head. "But I have to admit it freed me to become who I am. For better or worse."

Dina was conscious of her toe just touching Nick's foot, the barest contact, but it felt huge. Neither of them wanted to move for fear of breaking the con-nection. A pink-gold shaft of sunlight bisected the room at exactly the height of their gesticulating hands. Watching their fingers dance through the thick hon-eyed light, Dina thought, "The antidote to despair is to remember *olam ha-ba*."

"Olam what?"

"Did I say that out loud?" she asked.

"Either that or this stuff has done something pretty remarkable for our sensory receptors," Nick said. "O-what ha-what?"

"*Olam ha-ba*. The world to come."

"How can you remember the world to come if it hasn't come yet?"

"Just a little spiritual technology from Rebbe Nachman," Dina laughed, "badly paraphrased. He was this amazing teacher who saw how intellect and imagination can get in the way of truth. The idea is that you remember what is to come by experiencing the little tastes of a perfected world in this life." She stared at the window. "Like that sunbeam."

"Like seeing you again. A taste of a perfected world." Their eyes met, the intersection of hopes and fears.

Living in the imperfect world, Dina realized she was cold. Stiffly, she got up to look for her sweater. Standing made her conscious of having had to pee for ages. Once she came out of the bathroom, Nick had water going for tea, he was slicing bread and cheese. Ordinary time resuming.

"Coming down," said Dina, wistfully.

Nick's smile was sweetly sad. "Coming dow-own again," he wailed, imitating Keith Richards. "On the ground again, coming down again." Nick extended his arms like Fred Astaire and slow-danced Dina around the kitchen, humming the tune in her ear. His inner voice hummed along, sweetly. When he ran out of notes, Nick kissed Dina, softly, first on one corner of her mouth, then the other, and then on her lower lip. He stopped when she stiffened at the kettle's whistle.

"This is good shit," whispered Dina, hanging on. "Do you know where I can get some more?"

"I'll meet you in *olam ha-ba*," said Nick.

Chapter 4

After their first Clarity trip, Dina was unable to resist picturing herself as a double agent. She'd be at her desk at work, drafting copy for a press release on some piece of legislation or a new program, but in the back of her mind she was plotting the launch of Clarity. She and Nick had agreed that discretion was essential, but they couldn't do all the work by themselves. They decided that each of them should select a single confidante who could help fill some critical need for the project.

For Nick that had been Gary, of course. That was a given. All their communication would be by computer, Nick told Dina; Gary's new obsession was data encryption. Dina had no concern about Nick's choice. Gary had always been as circumspect as one might expect a recluse to be: name, rank, serial number and not another syllable.

Dina, of course, had chosen Gabe—riskier perhaps, in terms of keeping confidences, but potentially at least as rewarding. Dina had hired him during Crayton's first gubernatorial campaign, giving him the title "Coordinator of Community Relations," which meant liaison with every organized and disorganized marginalized constituency: youth, people of color, gays, environmentalists. Gabe's joke was that hiring him had been one-stop shopping; as a black gay community organizer specializing in environmental justice issues, his qualifications were unbeatable.

Gabe was only twenty-eight now, but even at twenty he had known just about everything about spreading a message and getting people on your team. He had a million friends and contacts, and relied so heavily on access to them that he still block-printed an old-fashioned Rolodex card for every entry in his Palm Pilot, terrified that the information might otherwise succumb to an electronic glitch or spent battery. Gabe always said it wasn't necessary to get everyone on your side—just the people that everyone listened to, and he tended to know who they were.

Along with practically every executive who worked in their office, neither Gabe nor Dina had time for what most people would consider a personal life. Instead of dates, they dragged themselves at the last possible moment to indifferent restaurants near the capitol, consuming double martinis and hamburgers that tasted of charcoal lighter, dissecting their coworkers, their press contacts, and as they got to know each other better, the governor and his thwarted but still tantalizing promise. On weekends, they fell into some stupid movie. Like teenagers, they sized up the actors onscreen and their fellow audience members and anyone who happened to be walking down the street. Like teenagers, they were mostly words and very little action. Neither of them had the energy for small talk with civilians. Neither of them had a drop left of the idealistic hopes that had fueled their journeys to Sacramento; and neither of them could stop running on empty toward the thing they'd once desired.

They'd worked together for years before they had confided anything of substance about their personal histories. Dina had never been much into telling her life story. She'd hated school, hated the neighborhood kids—and now she hated retailing what sounded like self-pitying complaint about a childhood that was basically okay, especially when compared to some of the truly horrendous family stories she'd heard. The Milners' saga didn't fall neatly within acceptable narrative lines. To the contrary, it threw people, lulling them with conventionality, then ricocheting off predictable meanings into much murkier territory: Bernie's unacknowledged rivalry with his father for Charlotte's heart; his unstinting, failed struggle to blend in; Charlotte's compulsive need to offer unsolicited and half-baked advice, driving away friends. Telling it, Dina tended to get hung up on Grandpa David, self-consciously aware of her inherited habit of romanticizing the old rogue and of the pain it had caused her father.

Like a couple in a Hollywood romance, her parents had passed away within a few weeks of each other. This had happened the third year of Dina's tenure at the governor's office. Relating that bit of synchronicity always elicited an attenuated "O-o-oh" sound, awe at the joining of hearts. But often that turned into a choked-off giggle when she explained that Charlotte had succumbed to a massive, unexpected stroke in Macy's, midway in the act of tugging a man's knit shirt off the pile on a sale table. Three weeks later, Dina's father had died in his sleep. Of "a broken heart," people said, but Bernie's doctor had told her that too much digitalis had something to do with it. Whether Bernie had consumed it accidentally or on purpose, Dina would never know, but Bernie had been a careful man.

Dina missed her parents, but it wasn't so different from missing them while they lived. When people at Bernie's funeral had said what a good life the two had shared, how much in love they'd been, she nodded. But she couldn't help thinking that despite their homely virtues—a "good provider," a "wonderful homemaker"—it had been a rather minor life, half a life. What if they'd pursued something more than comfort? She wondered how their lives might have unfolded if they'd been willing to risk more, if they'd focused a little less on achieving the perfect TV family and more on the wide world, the meanings beneath its surface.

In contrast to Dina's discomfort, Gabe's reticence about his family was grounded in shame, pure and simple. He hated to be pitied, he hated to see the look of horror on friends' faces. When Dina was finally permitted to hear his story, she had to promise first not to say certain things, such as, "How did you ever come out of *that* family?" She kept her promise, but no vow could keep her from hearing the words echo inside her head: Gabe should have been their shining star, a boy who had pulled himself up by his own bootstraps to become a man respected and consulted by those in power, one who made a real, substantial difference in ordinary people's lives. But in the crazy logic of his family, Gabe's triumphs had become his disgrace, their glow shrouded by survivor's guilt.

Gabe was the youngest of four siblings, two girls and two boys. His older brother had spent time in prison for armed robbery. Visits to Wilson in San Quentin had been a regular feature of Gabe's adolescence. His mother—Jacquie—and his sisters would spend half a day frying chicken and baking, then dress in their church clothes to make the drive across the bridge. When Wilson was paroled, the whole family celebrated. Less than six months later—a month before Gabe's high school graduation—Wilson was dead in another bungled robbery. Jacquie never recovered. The family living room was practically a shrine to Wilson's memory, while Gabe's achievements went unremarked. A glance at Wilson's photo could set Jacquie off on an hours-long crying jag, with Gabe and the girls taking turns holding their mother's hand, bringing glasses of sweet tea and fresh supplies of Kleenex to stanch the flow.

What Gabe and Dina had in common, at bottom, was their alienation. For very different reasons, their families were misfits—Charlotte's virtuoso displays of other-ness, Bernie's dogged simulation of a normal American, Wilson's downfall, Jacquie's inconsolable grief. And Gabe and Dina were misfits within their families: Gabe's exceptionalism as a gay black man, Dina's passion for justice arising from her parents' indifference. Both had wanted out of the little world of their families, and both had become adept at noticing and navigating what never even registered with other family members: the big world, its struggles and power structures, the nuances of culture and manners that enabled entrée.

They made a joke out of it. Dina said the only people she was drawn to were alienated oddballs like herself, the ones who had converted their alienation into empathy. Family names became shorthand for various life derangements. "He's got a case of the Jacquies" meant someone so sunk into his own pain he had become oblivious to others. "He-e-e-ere's Charlotte!" heralded a woman who was trying a little too hard to spin straw into gold. "A Bernie" described anyone trapped in the straitjacket of his public persona.

❉   ❉   ❉

Gabe had been nonplussed by Dina's fabulous tale of the new drug. "Whenever I hear the word 'clarity,'" he said, "I reach for my revolver."

"Thank you, Herr Goerring," said Dina. "What the fuck are you talking about?"

"Now, take it easy." Gabe held up his hands, palms out, in a characteristic gesture of harmlessness. His smile sparkled sweetly. "You know, when people talk about clarity, they usually mean some simple formula that explains everything—not. Like 'Let's be clear, this is a simple case of...' whatever."

Dina shook her head impatiently. "But that's just it. I hate it when those two ideas get conflated, clarity and simplicity. If people really saw clearly, they wouldn't fall for all these simplifications, these reductive little sound bites that pass for wisdom in the information age. If they saw clearly, they'd see complexity, because that's what's actually there, not some black-and-white sketch that imposes a simple shape on reality."

"Okay, okay, point taken," Gabe said, smoothing his shirtfront. He adored Hawaiian shirts—even though he'd not yet made it to the islands. Today's version had little blue guitars and surfers on a yellow ground. "So let me be sure I get the whole exquisitely complex picture. You're fed up with politics. I can see that, I really can, mm-hmm. So you figure, What the hell? You're just going to cube the water supply with this new Clarity. Okay. Okay. And then while everybody is wide-awake the Age of Aquarius will dawn. Is that it? Have I got that right?"

"No. We're not going to cube anybody. We're going to get them to take it voluntarily." Dina spread her hands and smiled, one-two-three. The tiny surfers smiled back.

"Okay," Gabe swallowed a big slug of his martini. "Okay. Fair enough. And how exactly are *we* going to do that? Tell them it's a diet drug?"

"So you're in!" Dina slapped her hand on the table, making their olives bob and tremble.

Gabe tilted his head to one side, looking as sober as Dina had ever seen him: long cheeks flattened, thick brows knitted. "You're serious about this thing, honey. Aren't you?"

"Yes, Gabe, I am entirely in earnest. This isn't a joke. I'm asking you to be my partner on this, help me orchestrate the launch." She smiled. "You know, having your finger on the pulse of youth and everything, figuring out how to make it happen."

"I haven't had my finger on the pulse of youth—or the anything else of youth—for a long time, girl." Gabe patted the expanse of forehead encroaching on his neat cap of dreads. "But I do know a thing or two about the flow of information on that great virtual highway of bytes and bits. If I do say so myself."

"Precisely my point. And I'm asking you to help me navigate, and if you tell a single soul about this, I am out on the street, on my ass, in two seconds flat."

Gabe put an imaginary key to his lips and made a locking motion. "I know how to keep a secret, Dina, so don't let that worry you. Plus I'm not about to broadcast something that could get me locked up. Obviously. And while we're on the subject, I'm not even considering doing something that could *actually* get me locked up, is that clear? And anyway, in this case, I don't even understand what the secret is, so if I tried to tell it, I'd lose my last shred of credibility. So it's definitely safe with me, I can promise you that." He drained his glass. "But could you just run it past me again before I make any promises, now that I know you're for real? In a manner of speaking, because how real is this conversation?"

Gabe had heard a little something about Nick, because the first three years they'd worked together, Nick had still been part of Dina's life, though never seen in Sacramento in the flesh. Swearing Gabe to secrecy yet again—just to be sure—Dina now told him the rest, all about Nick's commerce in banned substances, her Gandhi epiphany, the plans that were underway to perfect Clarity, and if they succeeded, to launch it.

While Dina waited, holding her breath, Gabe spread his hands on the little table, peering as if to read a message between his long fingers. It was kind of cool seeing Dina so jazzed, and truth be told, he could stand a little excitement. Besides, this was such a whacked-out idea, he doubted it would come to anything. And she wasn't asking him to become a drug dealer or anything overt like that, just to provide a little organizing advice.

"And we can't get into serious trouble, right?"

Dina chewed her gin-soaked olive thoughtfully. "I really don't think so. It seems pretty foolproof. Nick assures me we can be completely anonymous, and since Clarity isn't a controlled substance, they can't bust us for it even if they know who we are, which they can't. LSD was in circulation for a long time before it became illegal; MDMA too. They'd probably act faster now, but not that fast. I mean, I'm not a daredevil. You know me. I wouldn't do it if I thought they could get us, right?"

"Probably not," said Gabe, peering from behind lowered lids. "But let's just say my trouble-o-meter is a little finer-tuned than yours. Have you ever seen San Quentin?"

"Just driving past."

"And that's all you want to do, if you catch my drift." Gabe sighed.

"I get that, Gabe. But if you were as paranoid as you make out, you'd be spending your days adding up columns of figures or something and your nights with a wife and two-point-five kids. Instead, you're out and about as an activist. It isn't like you've chosen the safest and least conspicuous lifestyle."

"No," said Gabe. "My principle has always been maximum safety within maximum realness. You know? I mean, yeah, poor Wilson was one kind of negative example. Do not want to get locked up, do not want that. But Jacquie is another—where you're free, but your life is a kind of sacrifice to something that doesn't give a damn about sacrifices. If I played it totally safe, I might as well be dead. But that doesn't mean I'm about to commit a major, public felony. Subtle distinction, I know, but I bet you can wrap your mind around it."

"You know I can." Dina raised her hand in gesture associated with the Girl Scout pledge. "Maximum safety within maximum realness. Our motto."

"Okay," said Gabe, high-fiving her, the sparkle back in his eyes. "Call me crazy—and, you know, I probably am crazy—but I'm in. I mean, oh well, I didn't really want to keep this job anyway. If we mess up, at least I will have found a way to leave. And if we make it work, this job could be a lot more fun. So it's a veritable win-win, *n'est-ce pas?*"

"*Mais oui,*" Dina said, taking his hand in hers and squeezing hard. "Win-win."

❦   ❦   ❦

Gabe's plan for the launch was brilliant. To share it with Dina, he created an elaborate PowerPoint presentation of arrow-filled flow charts, basing it on a sociologists' diffusion model used to map the spread of an epidemic.

Parodying social-science jargon, Gabe made up funny labels for the groups they wanted to reach: Intrepids, Early Ingesters, In-Crowd-ibles, Wannabes, and Whatevers. The idea was to get to the most adventurous people—the Intrepids—whom he saw as politicized students and young artists and activists. If they got a whiff of something good, especially something with social-change potential, they'd talk it up to the Early Ingesters, who'd basically eat any substance that sounded psychoactive. From there it would spread through clubs and protest rallies to the In-Crowd-ibles, the people who liked to think of themselves as hip, but actually couldn't catch a trend until its second or third wave had breached. Those first three categories included a lot of writers, media people, and other plugged-in networkers. With the kind of buzz they'd give it, Clarity would be tried by the Wannabes, the hipper forty- and fifty-somethings—trickling up, as it were, to the baby boomers of Dina's and Nick's generation who nursed fond counter-cultural hopes in some seldom-visited corner of their aging hearts. Anything after that was lagniappe—the Whatevers. If Clarity was widely touted as a good thing, anyone might jump on it eventually. What was most important was to get an influential and critical mass interested early.

Their distribution scheme was the simplest possible: since Clarity wasn't illegal, they planned to send it through the mail. The tabs would be simple, just plain, round white pills stamped with a C. Dina was supposed to stock up on jiffy bags, and Nick said it would be a snap to package the tabs in flat boxes, so that from the outside it would look as if they'd been mailing CDs or small books, something like that. Gabe thought it would be easy to get contacts from Intrepids out here on the western edge who knew folks in other parts of the country, and that would establish the core of the Clarity distribution network.

Gabe reckoned the plan would take about six months to implement, though it could conceivably go faster. These days, either something caught on or it didn't. There wasn't much lag time. To succeed, they had to create a wildfire. With Northern California as its epicenter, Gabe expected it would blaze pretty fast.

Dina was ready to strike the match. She was too old to make herself conspicuous in the clubs or at the anti-globalization rallies without evoking suspicion, so they had to get to a younger crowd first. Gabe was going to help them find a few contacts to start it off. He didn't want to come on like Mr. Pusher Man, of course, so step one was to be elaborately casual: tell some close friends he'd been given this new thing, way more interesting than X, and did they want to trip with him and check it out? Based on what Dina had told him, he expected that once they'd had a taste they'd want more, and that would ignite the spark. But he had to see for himself, of course.

His test-run was on a Saturday night. Dina had breakfast on the table when he showed up the next morning to report.

Standing at the door, Gabe looked sleek and happy, like a lion after the hunt. His dark face shone: long nose, delicate chin, cheeks curving upward. The birds of paradise on his shirt glowed brightly. Stepping into the house, he inhaled the cozy scents of something toasting, of coffee brewing. "Colonel Pryor reporting, ma'am," he saluted.

"At ease, Colonel," said Dina, letting him pass. "Hey, what do I have to be to outrank you?"

"Captain, like on *Star Trek*."

"All right!" said Dina, standing a little straighter as she poured orange juice. "So tell me why you look so happy." She longed to hear that Gabe's experience had matched her own.

"Funny thing about that. I was thinking about something on the way over. Like if I was selling this, I think I'd see a big payday coming my way. Let's see, even a buck a hit times a few million…Well, just do the math. But we aren't selling it, are we, Captain my captain? Because we alienated oddballs are straight arrows, so to speak, aren't we?"

Dina was dumbfounded. "I guess we're not selling it. You know, it seems idiotic, but Nick and I never talked about money. Why, do you think we have to sell it to make it credible? Like it won't work if it's free, the old get-what-you-pay-for thing?"

Dina didn't have a commercial bone in her body. If Gabe wanted her to see the potential, he'd have to connect the dots. But he wasn't sure he wanted to. "No. No, I may be going out on a limb here, but I imagine there are a few people out there who can get with a program of free drugs. I'm guessing, but y'know, it seems like that *could* just go over. I mean, we do have incredible, no-fail economic development potential here, but why should we let that affect us? Money doesn't mean anything to me. I'm perfectly okay just giving it away."

Dina felt confused. "I've got to talk to Nick about this, obviously. Who is paying for this stuff, anyway? It's got to cost something to manufacture C."

"Okay, Dina, glad I could bring this obscure little point to your attention. You ask Nick, just do that. Whatever the mysterious Nick says is fine by me. Why would I care about making a fortune when I could stay poor? I'm down with marginality, you know. Just shooting the breeze."

Beneath all the jocular patter, a flash of queasiness jabbed Gabe's stomach. This was kind of a big oversight. He hoped Dina and her partners had thought things through—very carefully. It wasn't like her to go off half-cocked. With anyone else, he would have asked every conceivable question before taking the plunge, but with Dina, it hadn't really occurred to him. Truth be told, he'd never known Dina to cross without looking both ways first—twice in each direction.

"I'll take care of it," Dina assured him, feeling a little dubious. "Right away. Now, though, could we rewind for a minute? If you think there's a fortune to be made, you must have had a pretty good experience."

"You could say that." Gabe dabbed some apricot jam atop the cream cheese and took a bite of his bagel, waiting to be coaxed. "It was okay," he shrugged, nonchalant.

"Just okay?" Dina tried to hide her disappointment.

"Mmm," he said, around a mouthful of bagel. Then, seeing her face, Gabe relented, his cheeks relaxing into a grin. "No, I'm kidding. Dina, it was amazing. Really amazing."

Dina looked relieved.

"I thought it was safest to do it with my support group, you know," he continued.

"Your support group?" Gabe had never spoken of this before.

"Yeah, you know. My buds, the folks who keep me honest. I mean, you'd have to be completely whack to think you could work in a place like the governor's office without some people on the outside to check reality every once in a while, right? Y'know, otherwise you find yourself acting all desperate and losing sleep over one word in an amendment to something that is so watered-down anyway it won't make any difference to anybody. Right? A person needs a support group for perspective, so you don't compromise what really counts."

Dina couldn't argue with that. She just wished they'd had the conversation seven or so years ago. "So who's in this support group?"

"Oh, the usual," he said breezily. "Gay p.o.c. who work for some progressive issue campaign and feel like aliens wherever they are. My kind of folks. Usually, we get together and eat some huge meal and obsess about how much we ate, and when it's just about time to go home and get a sensible amount of sleep, somebody brings up an issue that keeps us debating until the wee small hours. Just your typical, garden variety support group."

"But this time…" Dina raised her eyebrows, impatient.

Gabe put his orange juice down. "Girl, it was one of the most satisfying experiences I've ever had. The first hour was fairly normal—not so much eating, I think people were nervous about feeling sick or something. Just another night with the walking wounded except people were checking in about whether anyone had come on yet. Then, after awhile, we really started to talk, and I mean *talk*.

"The funny thing was, we usually sort of take it for granted that all of us feel like round pegs in square holes, twenty-four–seven. Someone makes some off-hand remark that speaks volumes and we all nod and mumble like the amen corner. We talked a little about work and all agreed how fucked up it was. But I can't say that was any different than usual—y'know, the scales fall from our eyes every week, and I guess they must grow back, 'cause we keep on keeping on. What was different last night is that this was the first time we talked about what *we* had been doing together as a group, how much we meant to each other. We just sort of spontaneously got into this thing of telling everyone what each person had said or done or been that made a big difference in our lives. I couldn't *imagine* doing that without some form of chemical assistance. It probably sounds corny, I know, but it was one of the most beautiful conversations I've ever had. No one wanted it to end, but when it did end, we still had the feeling."

"That's incredible, Gabe. That's more or less what happened with me and Nick. We said what hadn't been spoken. It was so real and intimate and satisfying, finally, to put the words out there."

"Yeah, well, I haven't told you the best part yet." Gabe had that Cheshire cat grin again. He patted the birds of paradise on his stomach.

"You met somebody!"

"Well, no, not literally, since I've known these people for years, but in the tactful and euphemistically ladylike sense you mean it, I guess I'd have to say *Yes!*"

Dina looked stricken. "Oh my God, I hope it isn't some kind of aphrodisiac!"

Gabe stared at her. Sometimes the woman made no sense at all. "Well, let's leave aside the question of whether that is necessarily a bad thing, while we get to first things first. You've been holding out on me, girlfriend. I gather you and Nick did more than talk on Clarity."

Dina felt trapped. She hadn't wanted to tell anyone, because that would make it real. It would become other people's business. Then what if it never happened again? What if Gabe kept asking "How's it going with Nick?" and she couldn't tell him the truth, or she didn't know it?

Tilting his head so that his dreads swung jauntily, Gabe said "I'll take that tortured silence as a yes."

"Sorry for spacing out, Gabe. Just took a brief trip to my home planet, I guess. Yes, we did do more than talk, but I guess I don't trust it, so I didn't want to make a big deal out of it."

"Well, I for one can't understand that impulse at all. I mean, I think I might have read about it in a book sometime, but I'm just about the most trusting individual you'd ever hope to meet—not. Listen, I'll tell mine and you tell yours, and then we'll both go into the Vulcan Mind Meld and have a complete brain wipe. How's that sound? Pretty good? Okay?"

❦   ❦   ❦

Gabe and Lance had been washing the dishes, ferrying glasses and plates from the coffee table to the kitchen, Gabe washing while Lance dried.

"That was special, man," said Lance.

Gabe turned to glance at his friend's face. After the long night, Lance's amber skin seemed stretched more tightly than usual over the sharp cheekbones. His narrow dark eyes shone. Straight black hair spilled onto his forehead, brushing his eyebrows. Gabe found himself greatly moved by Lance's features, which seemed to pulse and glow as he stared. "Truth out," said Gabe, clearing his throat. "I don't know what I'd do without you...you guys."

"I really appreciated what you said about me." Lance usually avoided looking anyone in the eye, but this time, he met Gabe's gaze head-on.

Gabe was astounded to hear his own next words, flowing free and easy. "I meant it, Lance. You do everything with a certain style, instead of just plowing ahead like me. I've learned everything I know about negotiating from just watching you. And since we're being all mushy here, I'll tell you—cause you know I'd never say this if I was in my right mind, don't you?—but you've got grace, brother. True grace."

Lance kept looking at Gabe, his hand making steady circles, drying an already dry plate. "And you," he said. "All those jokes and self-deprecating remarks. You make everyone feel easy, even in tough situations. I don't know how to explain it—it's kind of self-sacrificing, but in a good way. Graceful."

There was a low murmur of voices from the next room, and above it, the high, musical trill of water running into the sink. But all Gabe could hear was the pounding of his own heart.

Lance set down the plate, putting his hand on Gabe's cheek. "Nothing ventured, nothing gained," he whispered, laying his hand along Gabe's jaw and bringing his mouth to Gabe's lips.

The kiss shot to the tips of their toes, drawing their bodies together as if magnetized. Instantly, they'd pulled apart without a word, busying themselves with the dishes until the others had left.

Then it had been perfect, Gabe told Dina, like something out of a movie. "I've never felt so close to anyone. We made love with our eyes open, in every way, and even our eyes burned. I don't have the words for it. I can hardly stand to think about it.

"So," he said, clearing his throat and picking up his cup, "it's your turn. Do tell."

"Pretty much the same thing," she said, "except no support group and no dishes."

"Oh, no, Miss Thing. You aren't going to get away with that. Details, I need details."

Dina sighed. She wasn't a prude, but she hated to talk about sex unless she happened to be having sex with her conversation partner at the time. Probably having been born in the Fifties: she didn't have the words for it. Charlotte had told her the facts of life by giving her a little book full of clinical line drawings and words like "penis" and "vagina." Those terms seemed too scientific and cold, the others too crude.

"It was beautiful," she told Gabe. "We danced, and then it felt natural to kiss, and after that it seemed natural to kiss lying down in bed, where it seemed natural to take off our clothes, and then it was very strange and wonderful. He felt completely known and completely new. I recognized his body, if you know what I mean, but it was like having a very unfamiliar conversation with a very old and comfortable friend: exciting, a little strange, but safe in some deep, deep way. It was beautiful."

"Like a train going through a tunnel in the Swiss Alps," said Gabe, gazing wistfully into the distance.

Dina threw a piece of bagel at him.

"Thank you, Captain," he said, "I was feeling a little peckish. I don't know why you're concerned about the aphrodisiac thing. Seems like a selling point to me."

"I'm concerned because this can't induce any false feeling or we'd be defeating our purpose. I'd be concerned if it was anger or energy or any other feeling."

"Well, I wouldn't worry, then," said Gabe.

"Why?"

"Well, did you suddenly feel swept away by lust? Like you could have jumped anything in the vicinity?"

"No," said Dina. "I wasn't conscious of feeling sexy until things started happening between us."

"Well, me too. So, I'm not a certified expert, but I would venture to say it's not the drug. It seems to me the Clarity opened up a space for connection, and well, we just walked into it. But what do I know?"

"Plenty, my friend. You're right." She sighed, relieved, and poured them fresh coffee. "So did people want more?"

"Is the bear Catholic? Does the Pope shit in the woods?"

"The game's afoot," said Dina. They clicked coffee cups.

❧   ❧   ❧

The thing about starting with West Coast Intrepids and Early Ingesters was that Clarity didn't lead to any hugely noticeable change in their behavior.

Before C, they'd related to the mainstream society in three ways: avoid its authority, consume its products, and protest its policies. After C, none of this had changed. Dina brought the problem up with Gabe—he'd called it "cubing the choir"—but he just said to be patient and watch the signs, that soon they'd reach the point where it broke on through to the larger society.

Thanks to advice from Gary, Nick now had a top-of-the-line wireless computer set-up, so when Dina arrived at his place for the weekend, they googled "Clarity" and "drug" and got hundreds of hits. Someone had opened up an off-shoot of an Ecstasy site where people chronicled their trips. They read page after page of gee-whiz prose:

> **Overall effect:** Trippy **Physical effect:** Slightly blurred vision
> **User reports:** One Word: AWESOME!!!!!! I took 2 within an
> hour at about 11 pm and did not START coming down until
> 7am, about 9am it was gone. Great pill, I recommend it to
> anyone!!!!

Dina found this depressing. They hadn't set out to give people a meaningless good time. The idea had been to help them manifest awareness, to see things clearly. "I wonder if I didn't fall for my own propaganda," Dina said. "I thought that if people could wake up to the world around them, they would behave differently in relation to it."

Thank you, Pollyanna, said Nick's inner voice. But Nick himself was far from depressed. "Maybe," he said. "We don't know yet. Most of these people in the first wave are not well-set-up to behave in any way that truly has social impact." He gestured at the computer screen. "Most of these people are kids who got something in the mail from other kids. We've got to wait for the next wave."

"I know you're trying to make me feel better," said Dina, "but I don't really want to go down in history for having given drugs to kids."

"I thought the plan was to avoid going down in history at all," Nick said. Certainly he had no yen for publicity.

"And speaking of giving," Dina said, "Gabe just asked me about money. Kind of an obvious question, hmm? I felt like a dolt for not asking about it myself." Privately, Dina wondered whether this major oversight was some kind of default to her old way of relating to Nick: trusting that he'd take care of things without looking too hard at how. Indeed, entertaining that hypothesis had made her feel so creepy she had to admit to herself it was probably true. "Gabe thought we could hawk Clarity," she continued, "as some kind of economic development scheme for worthy causes and make a fortune. Are we giving it away? I mean, it's fun making up those little postpaid jiffy bags, but if this is going to get out widely enough to affect things, can we keep doing it that way?"

Nick had known this would come up—sooner than it had, he'd thought. "Yes," he told Dina, looking sheepish. "I want to give it away. What you said about making a *tikkun*?" Nick sighed. "Dina, I'll put it to you straight. I have more than enough money for this lifetime and a few others. Guys like me, we don't pay taxes. I guess most people in my position feel great about ripping off the government—and it isn't as if I want to put more tax money at George W. Bush's disposal, I don't see what's so noble about that. But it's not right to give nothing back. I woke up to that slice of truth not long after you left. Being alone gave me lots of time to examine my misspent life."

Nick rubbed his face wearily. "Mostly, I've been doing cash gifts to worthy causes—going to events where they take up a collection and slipping a whole lot into the hat, or getting blind money orders, the kind that can't be traced. So I can afford this. And truly, this stuff costs very little to manufacture. If Clarity is supposed to repair something, I don't think we can get it mixed up with commerce. Besides, taking in money means setting up a network to receive it, which means the whole thing can be traced back to us much more easily that way." He looked at Dina squarely now. "Does that make sense?" *Or will she think I'm a wuss?*

Dina nodded, putting her arms around his neck to lay her ear next to his heart, listening to the soft, regular thump.

❖   ❖   ❖

One Friday night a month, Dina and a few women she knew had a sort of *havurah*—a circle of friends who celebrated Shabbat together. They didn't do it in a very formal way. It was potluck, the hostess cooking a main dish and the rest bringing challah and wine, salad and dessert. Before they lit the candles that inaugurated Shabbat, they usually began by talking about their week. The aim was to let go of business so they could enter into a time of pure being. Of course, Dina's work seldom allowed her an entire Saturday off—she was lucky just to get through Friday dinner without an urgent phone call, let alone the whole of the following day. But she looked forward to it every week, there was something different about dedicating every seventh day just to being alive instead of getting and spending and making and doing.

It was traditional to sing on Shabbat, lifting one's spirits with upraised voice. Dina and her friends had written their own theme song to start off each dinner, sung to the tune of "Let It Snow," with apologies to Sammy Cahn and Jules Styne. It was stapled into their own little songbook, along with more conventional songs, prayers and blessings.

Let It Go! Let It Go! Let It Go!
Oh, the e-mail and phone's been frightful,
But the company's so delightful.
In the Shabbos lights' radiant glow—
Let It Go! Let It Go! Let It Go!
Since it hasn't shown signs of stopping,
All month we've been a-mopping.
With the help of our second soul—
Let It Go! Let It Go! Let It Go!
There's no need now to worry,
All troubles will surely scurry.
As we bask in the Divine flow—
Let It Go! Let It Go! Let It Go!

Legend had it that on Shabbat, a *neshama yetirah*, a second soul, entered each person, bringing a double dose of divine joy. Sometimes, Dina thought she could feel it.

When she was growing up, her family hadn't done anything special for Shabbat. For modern and mostly secular Jews like her parents, Saturday was errand day. But that turned time into what it still was for too many people she knew: a spool of yard goods. You could chop off a day or a week or month, and all of it would be pretty much the same. Shabbat took you away from ordinary time, introducing a rhythm to the temporal landscape. The more Dina did it, the more it meant to her.

Dina's friend Nancy taught history at Sacramento State. She'd arrived at the door talking a blue streak, and hadn't shut up since. "I don't know what it is," she told the others, her eyes huge, her hands moving in the air, her cloud of graying blonde hair vibrating, "but something about them has changed. It's like the whole school is on a mood swing."

"Maybe they're putting hormones in the water," said Ronnie, tight cap of black curls bouncing as she swiveled her head, looking to the others for acknowledgement. "I know they generally account for my mood swings."

"Like what kind of mood swing?" Dina tried to keep her tone level, hoped she'd succeeded.

Nancy laughed. As she adjusted her shawl, a dozen glass bangles clattered on her wrist. "That's just it. It's not like they're acting out or they've become little Stepford wives or something. It's like I'm falling in love with them; they've become the students of my dreams. You know how I'm always complaining that students today are so conservative and cautious? They take verbatim notes and ask if everything will be on the test and it's hard to get a real discussion going?"

The others nodded, having heard these well-rehearsed complaints before.

"Well," she continued breathlessly, "it's like all of a sudden they see the underlying issues, and they've been asking great questions, questions that lead to other questions, and before you know it, class is over and—get this—people don't want to stop talking! One class has been studying the history of immigration—half of them are first- or second-generation, but usually they don't have much to say about it. Keeping their heads down, I guess. But lately, it's been totally different. They were incensed at some of the comments from America-firsters quoted in our text, but it wasn't just knee-jerk stuff. We had a really deep discussion about the American paradigm: if it's a lie, if we aren't a haven for the downtrodden, then is there still a valid way to be a true democracy? Is it really democracy if it's just for the people who already have homes and security and a feeling of belonging? One of them read the Emma Lazarus poem on the Statue of Liberty—'Give me your tired, your poor, Your huddled masses yearning to breathe free....' I swear there wasn't a dry eye in the house, imagining the country where that could be stated with sincerity."

Nobody said a word to fill in the silence when Nancy finally stopped for breath. "And this very strange thing happened," she continued, "or maybe it's meaningless, I don't know. But at the end of that class, I was so in love with them, I said how great it had felt to be their teacher that hour, to experience their curiosity and clarity, and there was this huge burst of laughter. I looked around, I figured someone was behind me making funny faces, or something comical had fallen off the desk, but there was nothing. So what was so funny?"

Dina, who had a fair idea, said it was time to light the candles, so they all adjourned to the dining room, humming "*Shalom Aleichem*" as they went.

Normally, Dina would have told Nancy everything. They'd been friends her entire time in Sacramento. Other than Gabe, Nancy had been the first person she'd met who might be a kindred spirit. Mostly, their conversations centered on the shared kvetches of single women of a certain age; evenings tended to end on a dourly companionable note, with copious lashings of Ben & Jerry's. So it gave Dina special pleasure to see Nancy so excited, and would have doubled her delight to reveal to her friend the cause of her happiness. But security was security and promises were promises.

Dina put herself to sleep by repeating the bedtime prayer she'd memorized when she first began to brush up on her Sunday school Hebrew. Sometimes the syllables were comforting nonsense, and sometimes she mentally translated each word as she repeated it, turning it over in her head. Sometimes the beauty of the sentiment—to lie down in peace and to rise up in peace—touched her, and sometimes she felt like Pavlov's dog, having trained herself to trigger sleep with a certain sequence of sounds. No matter, the words worked for her. "Spiritual technologies," as she'd told Nick. Increasingly, she thought of Clarity in precisely those terms.

The next morning, she sent identical e-mails to Gabe and Nick:

> **The In-crowd-ibles have landed! Nancy tells me students at Sac State have suddenly grown hearts, brains, and spines. Time for a summit meeting. Noon, Sunday, be here or be terminally square. XXX D**

❦   ❦   ❦

On Friday night, while Dina and her friends had a delicious Shabbat dinner, a group of students from Nancy's class ate a supper of Clarity, apple juice, and pizza—in that order.

"It's amazing," Lee said, shaking his head, causing wings of straight black hair to float above his ears. "Like we live in two totally different worlds. I mean, when she said 'Clarity' and we all laughed, I thought, 'Oh-oh, somebody's gonna get jacked up with this. But she didn't even know what it was! How could she not? How could *anybody*?"

"Right, like your mother knows? She's into Clarity, hmm?" This was Tory, always ready to disagree, usually with sarcasm. Sneering, she toyed with the little ring in her right nostril.

Laughing at the very idea of his mother and drugs, Lee considered the problem. "I don't know, man. I guess if my mother never listened to our music or had a conversation with anyone our age, she wouldn't know anything about it." He laughed. "Because I'm sure as shit not gonna tell her. 'Yes, *mama*. No, *mama*.'" He shook his head again. "Still, us and them, it's like parallel universes, inside each other."

"Deep," said Tory, half meaning it. She pretty much thought of the older generation the same way, as forming a shell around her world that held it in without actually knowing what it was, just keeping the youth in check.

Brian cleared his throat. "I think the Clarity is starting to roll, people, because really, it seems funny and kind of tragic too. Like they love us— Professor Solomon, you can tell she is doing this teaching shit because she really loves it—but they don't know us. And quite frankly, I have to admit we don't know them either. And still, we're all trying to keep it real. It's sweet, y'know?"

"Yeah," agreed Tory. "Like most of them seem so unhappy. I see couples sitting in a restaurant, not saying a word to each other. How sad is that? I tend to think that's just what happens, it's like the flavor goes out of life."

"Not necessarily," Brian said, stroking his delicate red goatee, the pride of his freshman year at Sac State. "That's what my aunt Liz said to me—the exact same thing, how she dreads being in one of those couples who sit through a whole meal without saying a word to each other—and she's at least forty. I guess the general picture is that the generations can't really understand each other. And then there's some people on either side of the generation gap who haven't forgotten how to get there, so they can still cross over or connect."

Lee closed his eyes and sighed, letting the first wave flow through him. "I really wish this Clarity shit would make it across the great divide, because I would so like to have a real conversation with my father, you know?"

The others nodded, feeling Lee's longing as if it were their own.

"I mean, he can't bring himself to actually treat me like a person. I can be the good son when I do something he likes, or the bad son when I'm having too much fun, or just by telling him I want to be a musician instead of take over the restaurant. But it's like he believes I'm this *thing* he controls. He can just make me be what he wants me to be, and I'll snap right out of whatever I want for myself. He can't feature me as being a separate person with my own life to live. And this is not just whine: 'Boo-hoo, he doesn't treat me like an adult.' That's not it. I'm saying he doesn't treat me like a *person*, you know?"

"I do know. Because that's me too, but the other way around." Tory ran one hand through her tangled hair, then rubbed her eyes, smearing the black rims. "In this child development class, I read how before a certain age, children can't conceive of someone still existing when that person isn't in their presence. Like when you leave the room, you just don't exist. And then at a certain point, they realize you have a separate life, you are just somewhere else doing something." She looked at Lee. "Listening to you talk, it just all clicked into place." She let out a whoosh of air, like a jet-propelled sigh. "I just realized I haven't gotten to that point with my Dad. It's like for me, he only exists as a factor in *my* life. I never asked myself is *he* happy? Has *he* gotten what he wanted?"

"What would he say if you asked him?" Brian waited patiently for Tory's answer.

"Truth?" asked Tory. The others nodded. "I don't have the slightest fucking idea. Not the slightest. And that is on me." That jogged her memory. "I had the weirdest dream last night. I was standing on a phone wire, like a bird, and I opened my mouth and put my head back, and another girl came out of my mouth, all kind of slimy—like have you ever seen a snake regurgitate a mouse?"

"E-e-e-w!" said Lee. "I have! It was gross: this long slimy thing, coming out real slow."

"Yeah," said Tory. "But the thing is, the girl who came out was me too, and she was alive, and I thought, 'Shit! She's going to fall,' 'cause it's a long way down to the ground. But she didn't. She just kind of expanded." She looked brightly from face to face. "And that made me feel good. I thought it was like I was ready to come out of my cocoon, you know?"

"So maybe the generation gap is permanent," said Brian, "but it isn't like any of us have tried to reach across it. To be fair." Suddenly, his head seemed heavy. Propping it on one hand, he looked sidewise at his friends. "Listen to me. Like I need to be *fair*. Where is that coming from? This C is so fucking hard," he said.

"Word," said Lee. "But good hard, you know?"

"I like seeing more sides to things," Tory said. "But then seeing more usually takes you somewhere where you have to do something really scary, like actually talk to your father."

"Duh," said Brian. "Why do you think adults fear Clarity?"

CHAPTER 5

✿

Nick and Gabe hit it off so remarkably well, Dina kept having to remind herself that this was their first meeting. When she went to the kitchen to fetch fresh coffee, Gabe followed her to whisper in her ear: "Not bad, girlfriend. This gives me a whole new take on you."

When Gabe excused himself and headed for the bathroom, Nick made an A-okay sign with his thumb and forefinger. "Smart guy," he said, nodding, "good choice." *Like she's waiting for your approval?* asked his inner voice. Nick picked up his glass, distracting himself by staring into its depths.

The whole time they sat in the living room hatching their plans for the next stage of the Clarity launch, Alice the cat was stretched out on Nick's lap, kneading his thighs and purring like an outboard motor. Alice at eighteen had lost a lot of her agility and some of her hearing, but evidently her sense of smell was in no way impaired, as she was obviously thrilled to be back within olfactory range of Nick.

It was a pleasant scene, really: late afternoon light slanting through the windows spread a golden glow over the otherwise faded browns and rusts of the upholstery, over everyone getting along like a house afire. Dina couldn't quite say why all this bonhomie annoyed her, but it ever-so-slightly did. Things being easy always made her suspicious. When Gabe left, she busied herself clearing cups away, refusing Nick's help. She had that feeling of something brewing, like an oyster wrapping itself around a grain of sand, getting ready to manufacture a big fat pearl.

Nick and his inner voice debated what might be happening, but finally neither of them could stand the anxiety. He pried Alice off his lap and deposited her on the couch, heedless of her "O-o-owl!" "What is it, Dina? What's bugging you?"

When he wouldn't take "Nothing" for an answer, Dina tried to unearth the feeling. "I don't know, Nick. We're all just getting along like long-lost siblings and Clarity is opening the minds of the students of America and I can't shake the feeling of waiting for the other shoe to drop. It's just ominous."

"Why do you want to try and change the world," he asked, his face radiating polite curiosity, "if you don't really believe in the possibility of positive change?"

Dina was on her feet at once, furious. "What are you talking about, Mister Armchair Philosopher? I've given my whole fucking life to the possibility of positive change!"

She has a point, said his inner voice. But Nick held his ground. "I don't dispute it. But that doesn't mean you believe in it."

Dina started to answer, but Nick cut her off. *I remember this feeling,* she told herself, *banging my head against the brick wall of Nick's confidence in his own views.*

"Dina, listen to me a minute." Nick wore that look of infinite patience Dina used to find so infuriating: a smooth, all-American blond, blue-eyed mask that made her feel *other.* Now she considered for the first time that he might actually be patient.

"I just want to ask you one thing," Nick said. "If the whole Clarity thing had backfired—if people had bad trips, or it had the effect of closing down their minds—if Gabe and I hated each other, if it all went wrong, would you have any trouble believing that?"

"No," Dina admitted, "it would seem all too plausible."

"But the good news doesn't?"

A door opened somewhere deep in Dina's mind. "Oh, my God!" She rubbed her eyes. "What does this mean? Why do I have so fucking much trouble believing in good outcomes, and none at all believing in bad ones?"

"Well, I can think of a few reasons. If you called Charlotte after 9 p.m., how did she answer the phone?"

Dina laughed. "You mean *'What's wrong?!?'*"

Nick nodded. "So you are on the receiving end of centuries of genetic inheritance to expect the worst, and I don't think you can just leap over that. That's one factor. Another is more general: they say we were all under-validated as kids. We got attention when we did something wrong, when we colored outside the lines, but our parents didn't want to 'spoil' us—they thought too much love and affirmation would make a weak character. So all we really trust is the downside—we hunger for the good stuff, but we don't believe it when it comes. The final thing," Nick continued, looking pleased with his typology, "is more like a trick of perception, the old thing about the glass being half empty.

What constitutes the nature of reality as we understand it? Is it happiness disrupted by occasional misery? Or misery punctuated by short-lived happiness? If you think misery is the default setting, it's always just a matter of time before it returns."

"So what makes you so wise, Mr. Zeitgeist?"

Nick deflated, looking pained. His inner voice made a bitter, wordless sound. "Mmm," he said, "you haven't called me that for a long time. If you think I'm wise, you're sadly mistaken. I wouldn't put too much faith in me. What passes for wisdom is just a reasonably good memory for what I've read, and I've had a lot of time to read while the rest of the world goes about its business."

Ignoring Nick's stricken expression, Dina cut to the chase. "So you think Clarity is happening? The way we planned it? You think the news is good?"

"The news is never all good, Dina," Nick shrugged, pushing away the feeling that Dina had stepped on his toe. "But let's just say it this way: I predict even the bad news will tell us it's working, maybe better than we'd hoped."

Hands on hips, smiling a mile wide, Dina looked like an exclamation point topped with dark curls. "Last week Gabe called you 'the mysterious Nick,'" she said. "That was before he met you and found out what a fine fellow and an open book you are, of course. But if he'd heard that last answer, I think he'd be saying it again."

"Gotta keep 'em guessing," said Nick, picking up Alice, burying his nose in the soft fur of her neck. The inner monologue had become a rabble of anxious voices. Alice's loud purr resumed.

❧   ❧   ❧

Though Nick had made Gary his Clarity project confidante because of his expertise in drug design, Gary's obsession with computer privacy had also proven extremely useful. He had perfected a technique that allowed one to send e-mail from an undisclosed location, a false e-mail address that couldn't be traced to the existing sender by any known technology.

That made it possible for Dina to use her media maven chops to her heart's content. The only remaining obstacles to a full-bore media campaign were her own reservations. She'd always hated those rich-kid Sixties revolutionaries, like the Weather Underground with its communiqués: Bernardine Dohrn broadcasting, "Hello, I'm going to read a declaration of a state of war. Within the next fourteen days we will attack a symbol or institution of American injustice." As Dina saw it, their approach was shaped by the ruling class that spawned them, pronouncements from on high, all certainty and self-righteousness. They'd doled out their bombs like black marks, each punishment twinned with a crime: bombing ITT's Latin American headquarters to protest the coup in Chile, bombing the Agency for International Development to protest the war in Vietnam.

Clarity wasn't a bomb, and Dina didn't pretend to be a revolutionary, but still, she had to admit she was motivated by a sweeping vision of change that could easily slip into that much-parodied tone of radical grandiosity. So she was careful to keep it modest. She started by sending press releases to independent weeklies across the country and to a few local dailies that, due to the quirkiness of their own communities, could be relied on to run any story having to do with drugs, celebrities, or unexplained phenomena. On a particular spring morning, a morning so fine that Dina decided to break with precedent and read her newspaper on the front stoop in plain sight of the neighbors, one of these—the *San Francisco Chronicle*—gave them their first big break in its "In Crowd" column.

Take C and See?

Leah Garchik   Wednesday, April 4, 2001

CURE FOR THE COMMON COLD? Rumor has it that under the influence of new designer drug Clarity, Warren Beatty and Michael Moore have teamed up to buy a weekly slot on the WB network to feature humor, short films and short documentaries that tell the True Stories that don't get much network airtime in these days of Big Media. Tout Hollywood is buzzing about "C," which you can't buy for love nor money: you can only get it as a gift! Is that sweet or what? So what does Clarity do? Well, according to a press release TIC received this week from a group that goes by the moniker Vitamin See, this new substance enables the user to "see through false fronts and illusions" that "obscure reality," "awakening us to what's really going on." Doesn't sound like all that much fun to TIC. Without false fronts and illusions (and let's not forget adultery and plastic surgery), yours truly would be out of a job. C's not illegal yet, darlings, so if you want to try it, look out for geeks bearing gifts—they say Silicon Valley is all aglow.

After that, the buzz started to build. Gabe began sending Dina a daily e-mail with clips and links to stories that could have been C-inspired. It was hard to be sure, but many of these were suggestive.

For instance, the clerical employees at a well-known software firm compared notes, discovering that their bosses had been systematically denying them raises for the last year, citing the need for cost-cutting in a declining market. But these same bosses had accepted bonuses equal to at least a year's clerical salary. Management responded to these complaints with talk of the company's collegial culture and a raft of warm-and-fuzzy consultants. The employees fought back by leaking salary and bonus figures to the industry press in a memo entitled "Poor Little Rich Kids."

At Santa Clara University, a Jesuit institution hard by the Silicon Valley, students organized a forum on sexual abuse by priests. The general consensus was that compulsory vows of celibacy had a lot to do with the epidemic of abuse breaking into the news: all that suppressed energy needed to find an outlet somewhere. An astounding sixty percent of the student body signed a petition calling for an end to the celibacy requirement. The administration was facing a threat of censure from the Vatican.

Below each of the articles that detailed these events, Gabe had typed a big red C followed by a question mark.

❧   ❧   ❧

Passover started early in April that year, and Dina's Shabbat group decided to do the second night's seder together. Ronnie was in charge of the *Haggadah*—the little book that recounted the story of exodus from Egypt in the prescribed manner, so that the prayers and songs and ritual foods evoked the long journey from slavery to freedom. These days, there were all sorts of political versions—feminist, multicultural, you-name-it. Ronnie, who was a bit of a scholar, liked to mix and match, compiling her own edition. Dina hosted, providing the matzo and the symbolic foods for the seder plate. Nancy was in charge of consumables, cooking some things herself and assigning others to bring food and wine.

Dina thought the table looked beautiful. At its center was the seder plate she'd inherited from her grandmother, with the shankbone, herbs, horseradish and *charoset*—fruit-and-nut paste—in their proper places, along with a bright shiny orange, a new tradition. The orange represented inclusion in all forms, but the story that usually explained it put the emphasis on women: someone said that we need women on the *bimah*—women rabbis leading services—the way we need an orange on the seder plate, and feminists had taken this provocation as an invitation. This display was flanked by polished candlesticks, a vase of fresh flowers, a plate of matzo under its embroidered cover, all surrounded by Dina's good dishes and wineglasses. Each time the bell rang, the house was filled with new delicious smells and cries of welcome, the anticipation of conviviality.

When they sat at the table, Ronnie proposed they each begin with a *kavannah*—an intention—for the season. Passover was an evocative holiday. Some said the exodus from *Mitzrayim* (this Hebrew word for Egypt was almost identical with the one for "narrow places") was a metaphor for the birth process, for the child's arduous passage from the womb to freedom in the wide world. Ronnie shared a reading that associated the root of the holiday's Hebrew name, *Pesach*, with leaping, asserting that this moment in the Jewish calendar carried the potential to leap over problems, springing forward instead of going the long, slow way through them.

Nancy came next, drawing a deep breath before she spoke. She glanced at Dina, offering a quick nervous smile. With a clatter of bangles, she pulled a tiny enameled box out of her pocket and unfastened the catch, displaying the contents. "These are Clarity. Do you know what that is?"

Everyone nodded, impressing Dina. She'd have to make a note of that.

"This is my *kavannah*," Nancy said. "Clarity. My T.A. tells me there are no side effects, no weird visions, nothing to upset you. What I'd really like this Pesach is for us to get to the root of things, because I have some narrow places in my mind that could really use opening up. Sometimes I feel so constricted I could scream." She looked around, finding confirmation. "So let's do this, okay? I mean, if anyone doesn't want to, all right, no pressure, that's fine. But if just some of us do, I don't think it will spoil the occasion for anyone else."

Ronnie, always brave, was the first to reach for a pill. Others followed until only one was left. Nancy extended it to Dina. "What do you think, *bubbeleh*?" she asked. "Want to chance it?"

Dina shrugged and popped the tablet into her mouth.

It was the most interesting seder any of them had experienced. As they went through the order of blessings and songs and stories before the meal, Ronnie became increasingly mesmerized by the aptness of the words of the *Haggadah*. "I feel as if this was written for me, if that isn't too crazy."

"Well, you picked it, darling," said Nancy, arching her left eyebrow. "I assume it resonated with you. As we say in academia."

"That must be true." Ronnie stared at the letters as if they might dance off the page if she looked away. "But I didn't know it resonated *this* much."

"That's what they say," Nancy told them. "It's talking about us. We were all there together, standing at Sinai."

"I see it," said Ronnie, eyes closed, swaying. "The mountain, the desert plains, purple clouds on the far horizon." She inhaled deeply. "I smell the dust. I see myself standing in the hot light in a long black robe, my head covered. I'm going from group to group, talking with the children about what they've seen, calming their fears."

"Yes," said Nancy, smiling sweetly, blue eyes glowing. "I'm under a palm tree with the young men and women, helping them understand."

"I'm huddling with Aaron and Miriam," Dina told them, "trying to put it into words." She shrugged helplessly, smiling at her friends. "Once a press secretary, always a press secretary."

They fell without thinking into telling the Passover story in the present tense, as if it were unfolding right now, right here. They saw the horror of the plagues, sensed the precarious terrifying safety of being spared. They packed in haste for a nighttime departure, and cried for the loss of their homes, however humble. They felt that even slavery offered an embrace that was hard to leave, that even a divinely ordained journey elicited fear of the unknown. When the Egyptians were swallowed by the sea, they wept with mingled grief and relief. Closing her eyes on dry land, Dina felt the sun's heat thickening on her shoulders and the crown of her head, the hot sand sliding between her toes.

By the time they ate, everyone was talking so much it was hard to make space to chew. "I've been having a hard time the last few months," Ronnie confided to her friends. In the growing darkness of the room, a pool of candlelight illuminated her serious face, creating the illusion it was suspended in midair. "And I'm ready to be over it already. I feel that bad mood come down, and it's like having yet another visit from someone who's already made a pest of herself. You know the kind of person I mean? You open the door and it's her, and your heart just sinks. You just can't bear seeing that face again. But tonight I've been sitting here thinking, 'Ronnie, be honest with yourself. Part of you finds that narrow place very cozy. Part of you prefers the devil you know.' So I'm trying to open space in my heart, a big wide passage to let that familiar devil go out."

"And may you have space for something new to come in," declared Nancy, raising her glass so all could click, sending shards of golden light in every direction. "With me, it's about knowing somehow that we are all connected, and trying to honor that, and getting stuck in an old habit of pushing people away, creating distance. I guess we can't be saints, but I hate it when I notice myself doing that: I put my students into categories, separating the ones I favor with my great expectations from those I see as stuck in pigeonholes, the ones I write off as never going anywhere. You know? I feel myself react dismissively to something one of them says, and sometimes I wake up and ask myself how I would have responded to the same remark if it had come from one of my favorites. But not very often." She shuddered with distaste. "I don't notice nearly often enough. I hate to admit that, but it's true, and I don't want it to be."

"I've been thinking about something, walking around here at Sinai," Dina told her friends, her voice soft, large eyes round and shining. "When I was a kid in school, I remember this teacher looking at me and shaking his head. Thinking back to it now, I can see something in his face, like he could foresee all the trouble this was going to get me into. But all he said at the time was that what I wanted was reasonable—for people to do what they said, to behave the way they claimed to behave—but that people weren't reasonable, and they would keep letting me down. Today, I've been thinking how true that is, and how his saying it didn't change me the least bit.

"I still think the distance between the way we live and way we might live is so small. Really, it just takes a little turn to wake up and see that our actions have consequences, that we can't use other people like things. It seems so easy to make that turn—not that there aren't rough spots, not that there can't be a price to pay—but hey, there's no free lunch. You always pay a price, so at least use your ticket, take the trip. It just takes making up your mind. So why don't most people do it?" She sighed. "I know I sound naïve, but I'll tell you the embarrassing truth, ladies: I don't know the answer any more than I did when I was a little girl."

It was hard to stop, hard to leave, hard for Dina to let her friends go. Nancy stayed to help with the dishes. Dina told her a little bit about her reunion with Nick, but it was tricky to say much of anything without breaking her promise of confidentiality to the Clarity team.

"So you just ran into him?" Nancy asked, picking bits of turkey skin off the platter she was preparing to rinse. "Just like that?"

"More or less," lied Dina.

"So, how did he look?" *Let's get our priorities straight*, she thought.

"Great," Dina said. "Just like before, except little distinguished touches—gray temples, a few furrows along the chiseled planes, beautiful hands." She stopped, embarrassed.

"And how did it come to pass that you had time to notice the chiseled hands?" Nancy was eating a piece of sponge cake without really acknowledging it, absently ferrying crumb by crumb into her mouth as if she were merely tidying the cake plate.

"I don't know. We just started talking, and he invited me to the house, and I went. And one thing led to another." She trailed off, wishing she'd never started.

"And what did another thing lead to?"

Dina settled on a half-truth. "What you brought tonight. Clarity. We took it and talked about what happened between us. And how we could make a *tikkun*."

Nancy put down the cake plate, looking worried. "Is that what you want, *bubbeleh*? I thought Nick was a self-absorbed jerk who liked to sit back and criticize without ever risking being criticized himself. Isn't this the same Nick I heard so much about when we first met?"

"I don't know," said Dina. "Is he? Do we believe in *t'shuvah* or not? Can someone truly make that turn? Nick told me I must not really believe in positive social change because every time the possibility arose, I doubted it, whereas bad news I have no trouble believing the first time I hear it. So should I believe that Nick has learned something, that he's sincere? Or go with my ever-present hunch that no one really changes?"

"Oh, God, Dina, I don't know. I mean, yes, you should believe in change, or else what are we living for? People have to be able to evolve. But I'm just so worried that if you put your faith in the wrong person changing, next time you'll just be even more ready to believe the bad news and doubt the good. Believing that people can change and develop doesn't mean walking off a cliff."

Dina had a hard time falling asleep that night despite all the wine and good food and her bedtime prayer. Eventually she dreamed of being back in college, meeting Nick for the first time. She woke up wondering how her life might have been different if that first time had been the last.

❋   ❋   ❋

Signs of Clarity flickered ambiguously for a couple of weeks: lots of Internet buzz, the odd newspaper item, plenty of rumors—leaving Dina's thoughts ping-ponging. Was it really happening? Or were they making too much of coincidence? Then two things transpired to make her certain the Clarity launch was well and truly underway.

First there was the governor's annual encounter with the student dailies. This was a time-honored tradition. The capital press corps hosted a lunch for the editors of college newspapers across the state, and then the governor held a special press conference. Usually he talked about education issues, maybe announcing some new program or some special incentive for young voters. The college editors had fun impersonating real journalists, but no one took it too seriously. This year, though, had been a horse of an altogether different color.

Jeanette Woo—Dina had known her for years, from the old days in San Francisco—was one of the reporters assigned to cover the state legislature for a local TV station. She phoned Dina right before the press conference to give her a heads-up. "Whoa!" Jeanette exclaimed, "I can't quite get over the feeling I've been put on trial!"

"What do you mean?" asked Dina. "The kids asked hard questions about what it's like to be a grown-up reporter?"

"You could say that. How would you answer this one: 'Did you notice when you internalized the worldview of your employers, or did it happen so gradually that it never really registered as a change?'"

"Cuff me, officer," said Dina. "I'll go quietly."

"Exactly. There was one little girl with blonde curls who looked about twelve, so of course all the guys winked and nudged when she raised her hand. But they were really squirming afterwards. She pulled out an analysis she'd done of the main dailies' and networks' capital coverage, showing that official statements led over ninety percent of the stories. Only in around fifteen percent of them did any reporter ask people who would be directly affected by policies to comment on them. Especially when the people were poor or young, she said—like welfare stuff, children's issues—the entire debate was conducted between officials and experts talking about 'them.' Then she wanted to know why."

Dina cracked up. "So what'd they say?"

"Oh, you know, 'credibility,' 'reputation,' 'standing,' 'have to understand how these things work.' I swear Phil Carter almost called her 'little lady'—the L sound was halfway out of his mouth before he bit his tongue."

"I wish I could have seen it."

"You will," said Jeanette ominously. "Doesn't your press conference start in half an hour? Something tells me they may have a question or two for the governor."

And they did. Dina made the official welcome, introducing the governor, then watched from her accustomed place at the back of the room. She felt she could almost weep with the pathos of it: a bunch of twenty year-olds—more had piercings and tattoos than Shirley Temple curls, but they were kids nonetheless—behaving as if a press conference were actually an opportunity for open dialogue between officials and the guardians of the people's right to know. The governor didn't know what hit him. He'd read his prepared statement on a new tuition tax credit program that would cut the tax bite for parents with children in college, and the editors looked politely appreciative. Then they opened up with questions on almost every aspect of the governor's program. Prison appropriations created the hottest exchange; Dina stifled a giggle, recalling Barbara Hill's thwarted attempt in January to ask about the pay raise prison guards were slated to get while teachers were being cut.

"Governor Crayton," an earnest-looking young man had asked, "are you aware that 100,000 people are now in prison in the United States for the victimless crime of violating marijuana laws?"

"Well, I'd have to question your characterization, son," smiled Hal Crayton.

"Which characterization, sir?" The young editor held his notepad and pen at the ready, poised to record every word.

"'Victimless,' of course. As a 'gateway' drug, one that's especially appealing to young people, marijuana leads to countless victims."

"Could you cite your source for that, sir?"

"Please stick around after the press conference, and I'll have my aide help you with that." Smiling tightly, clutching the podium, Crayton turned quickly to the next questioner, a pretty blonde.

"Governor," she asked, "are you aware that total national law-enforcement costs for marijuana laws equal about fifteen billion a year? What would California do with the nearly two billion dollars decriminalization would free up? How many teachers would that pay for?"

Smiling rigidly, the governor sought Dina's eyes, locking on like a tractor beam. She knew what it meant: *Call this damn thing off, now!* But she felt as if her arm were made of lead. It took every ounce of energy she could muster to raise her finger in the "one more question" signal that would be implemented by the aide stationed near the podium. The aide was ready for it—more than ready from the look on her face—so she stepped forward immediately to tap politely on Hal Crayton's shoulder and whisper the traditional phrase, "Last question, sir."

Only this time, the governor turned to show the editors a long lugubrious face. "I'm sorry, friends, but Elena tells me there's an urgent problem I must attend to. I just want to compliment our institutions of higher learning on turning out such a determined and conscientious group of journalists. I wish I could spend more time with you. Thanks for being here."

"See you again soon, governor," called a young editor who hoped to be employed by Sacramento's fourth estate after graduation.

Crayton smiled and waved. Only his aide heard what he muttered under his breath: "Not if I see you first, sonny." He nearly knocked over the California flag stand in his haste to quit the dais.

Dina thanked everyone for coming and answered a few questions about how reporters got credentialed for the statehouse. Afterwards, the governor had called her into his office. He was furious. How could she let him be ambushed that way?

Dina's stomach had tightened at the summons. She suspected that a little Clarity had contributed to the student editors' stellar performance, which gave her the oh-oh feeling of a kid called to the principal's office. But then she realized Crayton couldn't possibly have known that. She played it straight. "How could I have avoided it, Governor?"

He pinched the thick tan skin between his eyes, struggling for control. A little cloud of smoky cologne wafted toward Dina's nose. "I don't know, God damn it. They were like a bunch of little computers with their numbers and questions. Whatever happened to 'How 'bout them Bruins?'"

"So, Governor, you're complaining to me because these students were too intelligent and well-informed? How about giving yourself a big pat on the back instead? The education governor?"

"Fine, fine, whatever." Crayton pointedly turned his attention to a rank of papers stacked on the vast blue desk blotter awaiting his signature. "Just see what you can do about keeping the marijuana stuff from being the lead story on the six o'clock news, okay?"

Dina felt about as ambivalent as anyone possibly could, like one of those characters in a cartoon who can't decide which way to look, so ends up tying its neck in a knot. She went back to her office to work the phones.

❦   ❦   ❦

While Governor Crayton halfheartedly raked Dina over the coals, the student editors sat in an Internet café about a mile from the capitol discussing their day.

"How stupid do they think we are?" Kelly stirred her cup furiously, still fuming about the cute-little-girl treatment she'd been getting all day from both politicians and the press corps. Under the blonde curls, her face was an alarming shade of red.

Jason wasn't sure. He had a wiry, street-smart look and a lilting accent that led almost everyone he'd met at UCLA to ask, "Where you from anyway, man?" "That's a hard question," he said, his brow screwed in thought. "I mean, do they believe their own bullshit? If they do, then they don't think we're stupid, they're just repeating stuff they actually find convincing themselves, you know? But even if they don't believe it themselves, then—still—is it that they think we're dumb and will swallow anything? Or are they giving it their best shot, and they've just lost touch with what other people will buy? Because—truth out, my friends—I don't think they're saving the good stuff for someone else. I think what we got today is what they're serving up, twenty-four–seven."

Everyone was quiet for a minute, taking this in.

"Okay," said Kelly. "Let's follow that one through to the end of the line. Today, Adam, when you asked that question about internalizing their employers' world-view, and they gave you all that bullshit about the diversity of opinion in the newsroom, did you feel they were telling you the truth as they actually believe it? Because I really doubt it. When I gave my analysis of quote sources and they fired back all that credibility and reputation crap, I couldn't believe anybody would think that was a good-enough answer to why the people they're writing about never get to express their opinions of what's being done to them." She banged her spoon down on the table. "I still can't believe it."

Adam closed his hooded eyes, expelling a loud breath through a wide mouth, the strongest feature in an open, sensual face. "I get what you're saying, Kell. I really do. It's crazy, but it would be better if they did think we were stupid and they were just feeding us any old line to get over. That way, they could know the truth somewhere inside, and there's more hope they could get in touch with it somehow. But if they really believe their own line of horseshit? Then where do we go from there?"

"Well, what are the possibilities?" Jason began ticking them off on slender brown fingers. "One—did you guys read *Candide*? I had it in French lit this semester—one is that they think they're doing the best possible thing in the best of all possible worlds. They're just convinced, you know? Two: they're outright lying to us. They know their butts have been bought and paid for, and they're ashamed to admit it or too cynical to care."

"Three," said Heather, tossing her long brown hair over one plump shoulder, "they have heard this basic concept all their lives, the free marketplace of ideas, the fourth estate, guardians of democracy, defenders of freedom. They like this job description, and they see no reason to torture themselves about whether it's accurate. They're just busy and doing their best and why hassle anyway?"

"Four," Kelly's green eyes glittered with rancor. "They don't know shit. They sincerely have no idea why anybody would be unhappy with the left-right spectrum of the mainstream news. They don't read the alternative press or Web sites. They actually think they're telling the whole story. Our adviser told us about this time she contacted NPR to pitch something about the Arts Endowment when the censorship scandals were in the news. A lot of grassroots community arts people weren't really supporting the NEA, and she wanted to do a piece on why. The NPR news editor told her, 'We already have both sides of the story,' meaning abolish the evil NEA versus save the glorious NEA. The guy was completely convinced there could only be two sides! So I'd say number four is stone cold ignorance."

Jason held up four fingers, then pointed to his thumb. "Five is that their interests as they see them just happen to be identical to their employers' interests—there's no gap. You know, they're middle-class, they want to be editors themselves or write big-time exposé bestsellers, they have their eyes on the prize, they don't want to do anything to upset the people who have the power to give it to them. It isn't that they started to adopt those views when they got their jobs; it's that they've seen their bread as being buttered on that same side their whole lives."

"Yeah, well, six is that if they don't do what their employers want, they're out of a job." Kelly shrugged. "But still, it shouldn't stop them from asking intelligent questions. Should it?"

Open-mouthed, pointing her finger at her throat, Heather mimed barfing motions. "O-o-o-oh! This is so painful. So the people who control this profession are either dumb, self-interested to the max, lazy, cynical, or just coerced or duped?"

"Or all of the above," said Kelly.

"Except for the ones who aren't." They all turned to Adam, who continued. "Well, obviously, the capital reporters for TV networks and major dailies—that's not the entire press. There are some strong voices out there. They just don't spend too much time looking at their own back yard."

"So this is what we're about?" Heather asked. "Our noble mission? We're the ones who're going to restore the role of the fourth estate while checking our assumptions at the door?"

Kevin had sat silently through the entire exchange, drawing patterns in a smear of sugar and milky coffee on the table. Now he raised straight black eyebrows, clearing his throat. "Clarity in the morning coffee? Make it part of contract negotiations?"

They all laughed out loud, Adam's laughter propelling a mouthful of latté across the table, flecks of foam just missing Kelly's lap.

"I don't think it's just about doing the journalism thing better," Kevin told them. His narrow black eyes scanned the table, connecting with each of his friends. "I think we have to go further. Much further."

"Like what?" Jason looked intrigued.

"Like this Clarity wave is obviously happening, and these people here in Sacramento are completely clueless, right? So, is it just going to be people having private revelations and asking exciting questions at press conferences, or do we do something to harness all this energy? And what about this network we've got here?" he asked, gesturing to his tablemates. "You link up our campuses, and you've got the state covered. Are we going to let this go?"

"Instead of doing what?" asked Heather.

"Look, what we've been saying," Kevin told them, "is that the hold-up is about these very basic attitudes. Like the things these reporters tell themselves about what they're doing and why they're doing it. I think we need to do something that goes to very basic attitudes about America: what we're doing and why. Like a new Declaration of Independence."

"We hold these truths to be self-evident, that most people go through life half asleep, letting the experts and power-mongers make all the decisions…" Kelly might have riffed her way through the whole thing, but Jason stopped her at the preamble.

"Not so negative," he said, dead serious. "I agree with you, but people don't have to buy our total critique to agree that something needs to be done." He gestured at the bank of computers across the room from their table. "Let's take a look at the original language," he called over his shoulder, already on his way to a computer station. Within five minutes, he'd pulled it up and printed it out. The table began to buzz like a beehive.

❦   ❦   ❦

After her meeting with the governor, Dina ducked into the gray-tiled ladies' room to splash water on her face. Standing in front of the sinks, Elena, the aide who'd ended the press conference, was conferring with two other young women: three sleek heads of razor-cut hair in the new style, two black and one red. When Dina came in, all three jumped to attention. Elena put her hand behind her back in a stereotypical guilty gesture.

"Smoking in the girls' room," Dina said, "tsk-tsk-tsk. Want me to tell the principal?"

They looked as guilty as if she were serious. Then Patti, Gabe's redheaded assistant, elbowed Elena, saying, "It's not *illegal.*"

Still looking guilty, Elena extended her tan, sturdy hand, palm up, to reveal three little white pills, each one stamped with the letter C. "One of the editors gave them to me when he came back to ask for the information the Gov promised," explained Elena, her round features in a tortured knot. "It's this new thing, Clarity, that everyone is talking about. And Patti's right, it's not illegal."

"Not yet," Dina said, "just like LSD or Ecstasy when they first came out. But it will be."

"See?" said Patti, the bright pink behind her freckles beginning to fade, "I told you she was cool."

"Thank you," Dina said, "I think. What have you heard about it? Have you tried it yet?"

"After work, we were thinking." This was Minh, a graceful girl who answered phones. "He said it was completely safe, and that it really opened your mind, but it wouldn't make you sick or act stupid or have a bad trip. You won't tell anybody?"

"Have you heard about it or checked it out anywhere else?" asked Dina. This was field research, after all. Gabe and Nick would be very interested in the responses.

"All we've heard is more of the same stuff," Elena told her. "And my boyfriend took it, and it was like they said it would be. He took it with his brother Luis, and he said they stayed up all night talking about what it had really been like to grow up in their house. He said it was amazing."

"Okay," Dina told them, reaching for the precise degree of middle-aged authority the situation demanded. "Because it's not illegal, I have no obligation to tell anyone, so your secret is safe with me. But be careful, okay? I'm not the only person who could have walked through that door, and some of the others might not be into fine distinctions."

❦   ❦   ❦

"Well, it's official," said Gabe, grinning from ear to ear and sketching banner headlines with his hands. "Student Editors Pin Governor to Wall," "Governor's Spokesperson Offered Drugs in Capitol Restroom."

"To be accurate, I wasn't offered any. Just let in on the secret."

"A mere technicality." Gabe smoothed his eyebrows. He was well-pleased with the effects to date of his information campaign. "This is the whole nine yards, Dina. I mean, far be it from me to be immodest. I'm sure my little efforts were insignificant and all—probably had nothing to do with it." He grinned. "But I don't think so! We kicked ass on this one! Internet, newspapers, television—did you see that 'Sixty Minutes' is going to do a segment on C next month?"

"And this is a good thing because…? What has 'Sixty Minutes' ever done for the good, the beautiful and the true? The whole program is based on the idea that everything has a seamy, self-interested side, right? To use an expression of my grandmother's—may she rest in peace," Dina said, "Fooey!"

"Well, to be fair, honey—and this is a little bit before my time—I believe they did give Daniel Ellsberg a little boost. Just a little bit, y'know. But what are they going to do to trash Clarity? We know there haven't been any bad trips or health problems. The stuff is being given away for free, so they can't expose evil moneymakers. I'm almost looking forward to seeing how they spin it."

"I'm not," said Dina, suddenly sober.

CHAPTER 6

Nick was the first to notice it. He had become addicted—"semi-addicted," he called it, being a man of moderation—to CNN, tracking Clarity's spoor. Now he was certain he'd spotted an unmistakable footprint on the national scene.

Dina and everyone she knew who was even mildly progressive had fallen into deep resignation about the 2000 presidential election after the Supreme Court halted the recount of Florida ballots in early December. Everyone knew that Bush had stolen the election with the help of his brother, Florida's governor, and Republican appointees—including his father's—to the Supreme Court. A bloodless dynastic coup. But Gore hadn't exactly covered himself in glory either. Dina thought the lack of persistent outrage said more about people's discouragement with the whole system than about whether they thought George W. Bush had the right to be president. But mostly those had been her private thoughts. The Democratic Party operatives who were thick on the ground at her office tended to position the whole thing in stark terms: "We wuz robbed!" Beyond that rhetorical trope, they'd had little to say, and Dina quickly lost interest. Her fatigue must have been shared, because the whole controversy had petered out so quickly. By March, it was barely mentioned in any public forum.

April, however, was beginning to shape up as a different story, and this is what had captured Nick's attention. A group calling itself the New Coalition had begun circulating a document entitled "The New Declaration of Interdependence," modeled on the founding fathers' Declaration of Independence:

> *When in the Course of human events, it becomes necessary for a people to revive the political bonds which have connected them each with the other, and to assume among the powers of the earth the station to which the Laws*

of Nature and of Nature's God entitle them, a decent respect to the opin-
ions of humankind requires that they should declare the causes which impel
them to such action.

We hold these truths to be self-evident, that all human beings are created
equal, that they are endowed by their Creator with certain unalienable
Rights, that among these are Life, Liberty and the pursuit of Happiness.
To secure these rights, Governments are instituted, deriving their just pow-
ers from the consent of the governed. Whenever any Form of Government
becomes destructive of these ends, it is the Right of the People to alter it,
and to institute better Government, laying its foundation on such principles
and organizing its powers in such form as to them shall seem most likely to
effect their Safety and Happiness. Prudence, indeed, will dictate that
Governments long established should not be changed for light and transient
causes; and accordingly all experience has shown that humankind is more
disposed to suffer while evils are sufferable than to right themselves by abol-
ishing the forms to which they are accustomed. But when a long train of
abuses and usurpations, pursuing invariably the same Object evinces a
design to reduce them under absolute Despotism, it is their right, it is their
duty, to throw off such Government, and to provide new Guards for their
future security.

Such has been the patient sufferance of the American people; and such
is now the necessity which constrains them to alter their former Systems of
Government. The history of the present President and the System that led
to his elevation to that office is a history of repeated injuries and usurpa-
tions, all having in direct object the establishment of an absolute Tyranny
over these States and their citizens. To prove this, let Facts be submitted to
a candid world.

President George W. Bush has flouted Laws most wholesome and nec-
essary for the public good, such as those governing elections and those pro-
tecting the public welfare and the lands and lives we hold in trust for future
generations.

He has refused to pass Laws to protect the livelihood and interests of
the great number of Working People, instead channeling the riches of this
Nation to the wealthiest Few, imposing Taxes on the people without our
Consent.

He has obstructed the Administration of Justice, by refusing to extend
civil liberties to visitors to our shores.

He has promoted as Judges individuals whose shameful records demon-
strate neither Impartiality nor a concern with the General Welfare.

*He has channeled public revenues in times of peace into the mainte-
nance of Standing Armies and the movements of troops without the
Consent of the people.*

*Indeed, he attained the highest office in the Land through sleight-of-
hand and trickery abetted by his Relations in positions of power and Judges
who are indebted to his Family for their good fortune.*

*The circumstances permitting these abuses were established by genera-
tions of Law and Custom, distorting our Democracy from general Liberty
into Freedom for the Privileged. In every stage of these Oppressions,
Citizens have Petitioned for Redress in the most humble terms: Our
repeated Petitions have been answered only by repeated injury. Our
Oppression cannot be ended by the removal of one Ruler, but that is a necessary step: a Prince whose character is thus marked by every act which may
define a Tyrant, is unfit to be the ruler of a free people.*

*We, therefore, the Citizens of the United States of America, appealing
to the Supreme Judge of the world for the rectitude of our intentions, do, in
the Name, and by Authority of the good People of this Nation, solemnly
publish and declare, that as citizens of Free and Independent States we no
longer recognize the authority of the Person who calls himself President,
and will take immediate Steps to Impeach him from that office and render
such improvement to the Electoral System as may be needed to restore
Democracy to our Nation. And for the support of this Declaration, with a
firm reliance on the protection of Divine Providence, we mutually pledge to
each other our Lives, our Fortunes and our sacred Honor.*

Reportedly, more than three million signatures had already been obtained.
Signatures were also being collected for several state ballot initiatives. If they
won, they'd direct each state's federal Representatives to introduce a bill of
impeachment, and if one had already been introduced, to vote in its favor.

The New Coalition never mentioned Clarity. Indeed, there was absolutely
no hard evidence that Clarity had played a part in the movement except, as
Nick put it, "Two months ago, the whole country was sound asleep. *Bush stole
the election? Oh well, what's on TV?* And now we have a new Declaration of
Independence? What else woke people up?"

❧   ❧   ❧

"Good evening," said Mike Wallace. "Since our program was created in
1968, 'Sixty Minutes' has reported on every chemical threat to the youth of
America: LSD, crack cocaine, Ecstasy, and many more. Now, there is growing

evidence that a brand-new designer drug is in wide use in America's universi-
ties, in clubs and at demonstrations—every place that young people congre-
gate. With a sophisticated distribution scheme that is based on giving away free
samples, the purveyors of the new drug Clarity—sometimes called 'C' or even
'Vitamin See'—have penetrated youth culture and begun to spread far beyond
it to adult thrill-seekers in the cities and suburbs. What is this new drug? Is it
harmful? Can it be stopped? Please stay tuned for a 'Sixty Minutes' report,
'Clarity: A Clear and Present Danger.'"

"Well," Gabe ventured, "I'm probably going all the way out on a limb, and I
sure hope it holds me, but my hunch is that they don't like Clarity. What do
you think?"

Nick raised his eyebrows, tilting his head in the classic gesture: *What else is
new?* From the outside he looked calm and slightly contemptuous, but his
stomach was in a tight, painful knot.

Dina was simultaneously unsurprised and disappointed. "Do they have to
be so fucking predictable? I thought Mike Wallace was for freedom of thought
and all that. You'd think he'd give it a chance."

"Maybe he will." Gabe turned up the sound. "That was only the hook.
Maybe the story will be better."

But the story was worse—much, much worse. The "Sixty Minutes" team
had interviewed a number of young Clarity consumers, all of whom described
the drug in terms almost identical to those Dina had promoted in her anonymous media campaign: it had opened their minds, they'd seen through the
lies, it had enabled them to say what had been impossible before. There were a
few aging hipsters too, and they corroborated these accounts. In fact, there had
been a professor who reminded Dina of her friend Nancy. She too had talked
about how wonderful it had been to teach since Clarity appeared on campus.
Someone even mentioned the New Declaration of Interdependence, sending
up a cheer from Gabe, Dina, and Nick.

After the commercial break, Wallace explained that undercover operatives
from his team had picked up an assortment of little white pills at various clubs
and other venues in New York. Now they were arrayed for viewers like a science
fair exhibit. Nick, the drug expert, ticked off the names as the camera panned
over them: "Man, these people are clueless. That's classic white cross there,
low-grade speed. That looks like saccharine. That could be Clarity, but the C
doesn't look quite right...."

According to Mike Wallace, chemists engaged by "Sixty Minutes" had ana-
lyzed the samples and come up with some surprising findings. Fully one-quar-
ter of the pills were garden variety speed, methamphetamines.

"Told you," said Nick.

At least as many were saccharine tablets.

"Yeah, yeah, man, you told us," Gabe said.

The rest seemed to contain no active ingredients at all. It was possible that they hadn't been able to obtain samples of the real thing, Wallace said, but these had been collected from reliable informants who had themselves consumed the tablets, describing their effects in detail. So that was the puzzle. Was Clarity real? Or just another name for speed? Or—most insidious and frightening—perhaps a preparation for something else, a way to get young people accustomed to free drugs, priming them for addiction to a far more dangerous drug to follow? For now, he advised parents to watch their children for the signs of abuse: changes in dress and appearance, marked changes in mood, sudden decline in grades, and so on.

"I don't get it," Dina said, clicking off the TV.

Gabe shrugged, causing his dreads to bob. The large dragon on his shirt-front shimmered. "You don't think it's possible that the trés-cool undercover operatives from 'Sixty Minutes' wouldn't have been able to pull it off?" He made his voice square and tight: "'Excuse me, sir, but could you possibly tell me where I can locate some of that wonderful new drug, the big C?' You know, call me crazy, but it occurs to me that maybe people would have said, 'Why is this guy asking me about C like it was this big secret thing when anybody can get some for free?' and just blown them off with some saccharine or whatever. Or am I completely off-base here?"

Dina feared he was. All those people willing to go on camera and say how great Clarity was—why would they balk at sharing one of the real tabs, especially when it was both free and legal?

"Or," continued Gabe, "maybe we're so cool we're already dealing with wannabes. Like how much genuine Clarity could there be in NYC by now? Maybe we need to spread the recipe around, y'know: 'Don't settle for anything less than the genuine Vitamin See.'"

Lost in thought, Dina barely heard him. She felt the back of her neck begin to tingle. Turning, she saw Nick watching her closely from beneath lowered lashes. Something didn't look right. Her heart sank.

"What is this, Nick? How come you're not making light of it like Gabe? How come you're looking at me as if I were a hand grenade?"

Nick was silent. His inner voice was loud, though, a sound of pure panic.

Gabe looked from Dina to Nick and back again, like a spectator at a tennis match. *What was this all about?*

"Nick, c'mon, spit it out. Is this speed? Or wannabes? Or what?" Dina's voice was a whisper, but to Nick it sounded as loud as a clarion, controlled fury spiked with fear.

"It's Clarity, Dina. Clarity is Clarity, and 'Sixty Minutes' is big business network TV bullshit, and why are you asking me to answer to Mike fucking Wallace?"

"Oh, I don't know," said Dina, impersonating indifference. "Maybe because it's network TV and a few people in our target consumer groups are probably watching it right now. Maybe because we just fell flat on our faces. What d'you think, Gabe?"

Gabe just stared.

Dina felt her eyes fill. "How could you do this to me, Nick? After all this, after all the promises and warnings it took to get back up on this damn horse after I'd been dropped on my head a dozen times, after all those years…How could you do this to me?"

"This is rich!" said Nick, sneering. "I didn't do anything to you! I don't know what the deal is. Maybe it's what Gabe said, maybe something else. But shit, you two have fucking taken it yourselves! You know what speed is like—I assume," he added, looking at Gabe, who nodded confirmation. "What is all this shit about changing people's operating system when you don't even trust your own perceptions?"

Nick stared at Dina, shaking his head. "I guess this is what happens when you spend your life spinning the government's bullshit. All of a sudden whatever Mike Wallace says is gospel truth? 'Sixty Minutes' says 'Jump!' and you say 'How high?' I bet you believe your own propaganda too. Shit, you go through the meat grinder and end up not knowing your ass from a hole in the ground. You *took* the shit, Dina. You tell me: was it speed?"

Dina felt blindsided—coming and going, Nick and Mike Wallace. Her voice got very slow and calm. "I don't know what to say, Nick. I don't think so. It wasn't like any speed I've ever had, though it has been a long time since I've taken any. But I'm starting to wonder about my own perceptions. I mean, I didn't think you were still nursing all this judgment about me and my work. I didn't think the first time I asked you a question you were going to spit all this high-and-mighty venom back in my face. So obviously, I'm no judge of what's real." She wiped her eyes on the back of her hand. "A lot of words, Nick, but only one question: how could you do this to me?"

"Fuck this," said Nick, turning on his heels and heading straight out the door.

Hearing the door slam, Gabe and Dina felt so empty they could barely move. Dina's heart throbbed like a blister about to burst. They tried to talk about it, but there was nothing to go on. Their lame attempt at dialogue was more like lobbing words across the room than forming real sentences, meaningful thoughts. Silence gathered on the dusty surfaces and lumpy couches of Dina's living room. In the end, hunger took over and they retreated to their old habit—char-broiled martinis and double hamburgers at a place with a hokey fire pit in the center of the lounge. But even that didn't help. How many times, how many ways, could they say they didn't know what to make of this? They ate wordlessly, left early.

Gabe felt that something ominous had sat down on his chest. Dina looked devastated, as if her best friend had died. Dropping her at the front door, Gabe tried to think of something light to say—his usual strategy for handling his own anxiety was to cheer someone else up. But all he could come up with was that old Scarlett O'Hara favorite, "Never mind, honey, tomorrow is another day." Dina mustered a weak smile in response.

The morning papers had follow-up pieces on the "Sixty Minutes" story, most similar in content (if not tone) to this gossip item from "The In Crowd" column of the *Chronicle*:

Whoop-C Daisy?

Leah Garchik   Tuesday, May 15, 2001

THE SIZZLE NOT THE STEAK? TIC is truly disillusioned: who can you believe anymore? According to Mike Wallace, the Mt. Rushmore of TV journalism, the earthshaking new drug, Clarity, is really plain old vanilla speed dressed up as the next big thing. And what about all those people who said it gave them the ability to see through illusions? Maybe they just needed a wake-up call.

That afternoon, Dina ran into Elena in the girls' room again. "So," she asked, hoping against hope, "did the earth move, or was it just a little old-fashioned upper?"

"I'm not a big expert on drugs," the aide told her, "but my boyfriend took speed when he was in college, and he told me it was nothing like this. That whole thing with him and his brother? Speed wouldn't make you do that. And when we took Clarity, it was pretty special," she shrugged. "That's all I can say."

"Oh, well." Dina shrugged too. "You can't believe everything you hear in the media, they tell me. And I've spun enough stories to know they're right."

❦   ❦   ❦

Dina called Nancy from work. "Cherry Garcia for dinner?"
"Oh, sweetie, what's wrong?"

"I'll tell you about it tonight, but suffice it to say the new Nick didn't last all that long."

Once again, it was hard to explain to Nancy without spilling the beans on Clarity. One of the voices in Dina's head said that if C was nothing but speed or saccharine anyway, what was there to protect? But Gabe had whispered to her that morning to remember that Nick hadn't really responded to the "Sixty Minutes" thing. He'd just said he didn't know. Maybe the problem was lack of supply. Or if Clarity wasn't speed or saccharine, what was it? They shouldn't make any sudden moves until they had all the information. Dina wasn't about to contact Nick to get the full scoop, so Gabe said he'd call and let her know what Nick had to say for himself. She might just as well pass the time mainlining dairy products with Nancy rather than obsessing about her disappointment.

Spooning up ice cream at the kitchen counter, Nancy looked properly sympathetic. She toyed with her glass bangles while she listened, favoring Dina with a sad, understanding smile.

"He let loose a stream of hateful stuff about how I spin the government's bullshit so much, I believe my own propaganda," said Dina, her eyes filling.

Nancy sat very still, suddenly looking awfully uncomfortable.

"Oh, shit," Dina said. "You too?"

"No, darling, no." Nancy patted her friend's hand. "It just that you've said as much to me yourself. Remember after that press conference about how Crayton is still 'the education governor,' how you felt sick to your stomach? And you said why didn't you just quit? And I asked well, why didn't you, and you just nodded and said 'Yeah, why don't I?' like I was asking why you didn't sprout wings and fly. But I meant it as a serious question."

Dina pushed her ice cream bowl across the yellow countertop. She leaned over and buried her head in her arms. "Oh, God!" she moaned. "Look, I am quitting soon—or at least this job will be over when the governor's term is up in January—and I'm not going to work for any politician after that, unless somebody like Paul Wellstone asks me. Okay? But that's beside the point. Nick has been all lovey and on his best behavior until now, and suddenly the lid is off Pandora's box and—surprise!—he still thinks I'm a self-deluding sellout. What basis is that for a relationship? If that's how he sees me, why does he want to be with me?" She peered desperately at the snapshots covering the refrigerator door, as if seeking confirmation.

"Look, Dina. I don't know where Nick is coming from: maybe he really doesn't respect you, or maybe the explanation is something about him, maybe he needed to lash out for some reason. What do I know? I'm sitting here like a moron speculating about someone I've never even met. But I don't think you're a self-deluding sellout. I think you're an able and idealistic person who has a tendency to keep trying too long after the cause is lost. You're good at telling yourself whatever you need to hear to keep yourself going. Like you still see the spark in Crayton. I believe it was there once, sweetie—I really do—but no matter how hard I try, I can't see it now." Nancy sighed, laying her hand on Dina's. "You know, there are those times in life when it's best to call it a day and let go of something.

"Like I always tell my students, every life has a narrative. There's some story we tell ourselves that pats all our miscellaneous and chaotic experience into a coherent shape. In your story, you're public-spirited, determined, self-denying, loyal, all that. And it's true—that is one of the absolutely true stories that can be told about you. But to hold onto that—to make it *the* central narrative of your life—you have to keep insisting that being the governor's press secretary is noble work, which is obviously a much more questionable proposition. So there's a big choice when it comes to life narratives. We can go through life in that defensive posture, fighting like mad to defend what we have and hold— but if we do, there's a downside: the story of our lives will be watching whatever we defend being taken away from us. Always."

"What do you mean?"

"Like women and our vanity, for instance." Nancy swept a cloud of graying blonde hair from her face. "So much effort, money, obsession invested in keeping something we inevitably lose: our youth, our looks, our sex appeal. You take that path—you choose to make that defense the core of your life—and what you're really choosing is the narrative of your self-defeat. The defensive strategy can never win. No matter what it is we're protecting, it will be taken away from us because—this just in, viewers!—everybody dies, and then our bodies and our positions and our possessions are of no use to us at all."

"May we both live to enjoy a hundred and twenty healthy years," said Dina reflexively, knocking wood on the seat of her kitchen stool.

"May we indeed, darling. But what are you holding onto here? Your defense of Crayton's integrity? Of your own virtue in working for him? Nick's presentation sounds a little harsh. I know it can't be easy to hear stuff like that from someone you let into your life. Anybody would want to avoid that kind of nasty surprise. All I'm saying is that what he said to you is what I've heard you say out loud over umpteen bowls of ice cream. And do we want the people we're close to believe our self-justifications without question? Or do we really want them to call us on that stuff? Maybe Nick really is a shit and he was just pretending to change. Maybe he was hurt that you were so ready to doubt him, and he lashed out. Or maybe you just didn't want to hear that particular truth from anyone's lips but your own."

"O-o-oh," moaned Dina, head in hands. "I don't think you were quite this direct before you took Clarity. Well, how about another maybe? Maybe I thought I'd learned a thing or two and I didn't want to be in this position again, making myself vulnerable to Nick's mighty judgment! How stupid am I? How could I let him in again?"

"I know, I know. How could you let yourself be dumb enough to want to be loved? What is wrong with you, anyway?" asked Nancy, smiling sweetly. "More ice cream?"

❀   ❀   ❀

Gabe reported that Nick wanted to talk with them that night. "He told me he has a whole lot of explaining to do."

"About Clarity? Or what he thinks of me?"

"Well, I'm just speculating here, but I'd take a big risk and say both. You think?"

Dina was deeply skeptical about whatever Nick might have to say. She kept fantasizing about treating him with cold politesse, believing none of his explanations, sending him away. But as soon as she imagined Nick walking away crushed, she wanted passionately to hear whatever it was he had to say for himself, to make sense out of this mess. The two scenarios dueled in her head as she and Gabe waited for Nick in the living room, saying little and clutching glasses of wine neither of them felt like drinking. Alice sprawled sphinx-style over a heap of cushions on the faded couch. The CD player shuffled through a pile of jazz standards, meant to be soothing. The atmosphere was unpleasantly familiar, like the waiting room of a dentist's office.

Dina answered the door. It was odd to see Nick carrying a briefcase. Quiet and contained, he looked far less like his younger self than he had appeared to Dina at their last meeting. His careful carriage seemed to embody the gravity of the occasion. The skin around his blue eyes was the color of a bruise, the chiseled cheeks seemed hollow.

Dina's face at the door looked to Nick like a barred gate. "May I come in?" he asked. *This is going to be harder than you could ever have imagined*, said his inner voice.

"Do I have a choice?" Dina kept her voice expressionless.

Nick reached his hand toward Dina's shoulder, but she stepped back. "Dina," he said, forcing himself to meet her lowered eyes, "I'm very sorry about last night. I was frustrated about that Mike Wallace shit, and when you started questioning me, my defenses went up. It was juvenile—I just saw red. I shouldn't have said what I said."

"Should schmood. The question is whether you really think it." Dina leaned against the hall wall, not giving an inch. She could see the embarrassing clutter of her workroom out of one eye. Even though she'd already told him she talked to his photo, she found herself hoping Nick wouldn't notice it on the shelf just above her computer.

Nick sighed. *Just put your head in this noose,* said his inner voice. *Might as well get it over with.* "Loyalty to Hal Crayton is not your most attractive quality," he told Dina. "And yes, I guess I think you do believe your own propaganda—that sticking with your job is somehow holding the line against the forces of evil. But as far as I can see, Crayton is pretty well compromised. Truth and justice aren't a big part of his concerns anymore, if they ever were. What I think is if you woke up all the way, you'd see that for yourself."

"And if I woke up all the way, would I live like you, matching your great contributions to humanity?" Dina's mouth pulled down at the corners, softness distorted into strain.

Nick's face froze. *Gotcha!* said the voice. He struggled to stay calm, to avoid getting hooked. "Okay," he told her, "I admit it. I deserve that. I'm not holding myself up as a paragon. But I guess I care about what you really think too. Do you have any respect for me at all?"

Dina was quiet for a moment. She wanted to lie, but she made herself tell the truth. "Yes," she said at last. "Yes, I do. I see you as someone who's made his own way and lived by his own lights and I respect that. But I think you see yourself as a righteous person, fighting the good fight, and the way I see it, most of that fight is in your head."

"I can't deny that," said Nick. "But I'm trying to repair it—make a *tik...,* *tikku....*"

"A *tikkun,*" Dina reminded him, against her better judgment.

"Maybe we both need to make one," Nick told her. "Are you denying that your own self-image might be some distance from the truth at this point? Crayton is no people's hero to anyone but you."

"I do see it," Dina admitted, sighing. "But I'm unhappy with where that leaves me. Who is worth working for, then? Nobody's perfect. If all the people who actually do care about truth and justice get out of positions like mine, wouldn't that concede the whole field to the villains who don't care about anything but winning?"

"Maybe. Or the truth-and-justice people could spend their energy making something important happen instead of fighting a million tiny fires. What could you have done with all the time you've put in at the governor's office the last seven years?"

"And you? What about the last twenty years? Where do you get off judging me? And how dumb am I to care? What an idiot I am!" Dina's eyes flooded. She blinked like mad to keep the tears from spilling.

Heralded by a throat-clearing sound, Gabe appeared at the end of the hallway, resplendent in a red shirt dotted with starfish and scallop shells. He had an uncomfortable expression, wrinkled brow atop queasy little smile. Had he gotten himself into some kind of soap opera here? "Just thought I'd mention that I can hear every word you're saying. Just in case you were planning to get to anything embarrassing. Shall I go?"

"Hi," said Nick, extending his hand. "I owe you an apology too."

"Maybe so," Gabe replied, "but for starters, I'd like an explanation. Maybe we can do apologies for dessert."

Nick marched down the hall, lifting file folders out of his briefcase as he went. He moved a glass vase of daffodils onto the sideboard, then arranged two long rows of papers on the now-empty Danish modern dining table. In the background, Johnny Hartman crooned "Autumn Leaves."

"Are we supposed to read all this stuff?" asked Gabe, stoking his delicate chin. "It looks like a briefing book waiting to be assembled and, y'know, that's a little too much like my day job."

"I suppose it is," Nick replied, very serious. "And yes, you can read it later if you want to, but right now, it's just background material. I can explain everything you need to know." He gestured to them to sit at the table, and with the air of well-behaved children, they complied.

"Okay," said Nick, rubbing his hands on his legs, "we have to start with the basics and work up from there. Now, you understand that everything material is made of atoms, right? The nature of a material depends on how the atoms are arranged. Like remember when Superman squeezed a lump of coal to make a diamond? If you rearrange the atoms in coal, you get diamonds. Following me?"

"No," said Dina out of the side of her mouth. "Couldn't you start a little further back, like 'In the beginning, God created...?'"

Nick's face twitched into something that might have become a smile, but he switched it off. "Just wanted to define my terms. Okay?"

Gabe saluted. "Roger that."

"Okay. So in ordinary manufacturing, as you know, people use huge clumps of atoms—like fastening one piece of wood to another, or welding two pieces of metal. As I'm sure you know, as technology has improved, we've been able to manufacture smaller and smaller parts, miniaturizing things like computers, cameras, and telephones."

Nick took a deep breath. Both Gabe and Dina rested their heads on their hands, boredom imminent, frustration approaching.

"Have you heard of nanotechnology?" Nick asked.

They both sat up straighter.

"Teeny-weeny little machines," said Dina.

"That's right." Nick glanced at Gabe, who nodded. "A nanometer is one-billionth of a meter, about the size of an atom. The idea is to create microscopic devices, no more than a few atoms in any dimension. People have been working toward that in many fields."

"It's a sci-fi staple," Dina said matter-of-factly. "You breathe in a horde of nanobots and they kill you from the inside. That sort of fun thing."

"Most experts have predicted that true nanotechnology—our ability to create nanobots—is a few decades off. Some people think nanomedicine is going to be the first breakthrough. Our bodies are full of incredibly small and complex molecular machines, like hemoglobin molecules or nerve cells. Those machines spend their time repairing the body on the molecular level. When things go wrong that they can't fix, we have to resort to big, clumsy tools— flooding the whole system with chemicals, or cutting into organs. Research scientists have been working toward the day when we can deploy tiny machines that work on the molecular level to rearrange the atoms that have become disarrayed or distorted. Like what if you could create a blood pump as tiny as a hemoglobin cell, and you could introduce a bunch of them into the human body, each one programmed to attach to a defective cell and restore or take over its proper functioning?"

"*The Fantastic Voyage*," breathed Gabe, "tiny Raquel Welch-bots."

Nick ignored him, or perhaps he was merely too wrapped up in his explanation to get the joke. "Like I said," he continued, "the body is already doing this for itself. Molecular machinery programmed by our cells' genes uses material it takes from blood to build biological structures like bone and connective tissue, like replacing damaged skin and healing other injuries. There is this constant process of tiny organic machines reproducing themselves and creating other specialized microscopic machines inside of us. Some of them ward off attackers, like virus and bacteria. Some of them run down, like when we get old, and that's why our parts don't get repaired as soon or as well as they were when we were young. Why we get wrinkles. The molecules of drugs that are prescribed for illness bind to other molecules already in our bodies and change their behavior somehow—they stimulate or suppress some secretion or other function, for instance." Pausing for breath, Nick gestured to the papers laid out on the table. "These diagrams spell it all out."

"I think we're getting the picture." Dina felt impatience and anxiety returning all at once. "I almost don't want to ask, but where is this headed? Let's cut to the chase, please."

"Okay. Here's the punchline. Gary has figured out a way to do it."

"Gary?" asked Gabe.

"Gary is my consultant on drug design, the way that you are Dina's consultant on viral marketing."

"Ooh," said Gabe, shaking his hands as if he were trying to get rid of a sticky pest. "I hate that expression."

"And he also happens to be the computer privacy genius I told you about," said Dina.

"Sorry for the jargon," said Nick, "but that's the point. You've perfected ways of getting people to spread the word for you, so it doesn't all have to emanate from one busy, expensive source. Gary has perfected ways of adjusting the brain chemistry that don't involve drugs as we understand them. Psycho-pharmacologists have known for some time that some of the most powerful and fast-acting hallucinogens work the way they do because their molecular structures are very close to a naturally occurring brain chemical, tryptamine. They are also aware—all of us are aware of this too, we just don't say it the same way—that the character of our thoughts and perceptions is dependent on the brain's metabolic state. So we have one type of thought in REM sleep, another when we're metabolizing LSD, and so on.

"What Gary has created is microscopic nanobots that, when ingested, bind to tryptamine in the brain and produce a state that we describe as Clarity. In simple terms, the background noise in the affected cells is quieted, and instead of a bundle of conflicting impulses and constantly varying chemical influences, our brains temporarily become focused on those things in our environment or consciousness we perceive as ultimately significant. The nanobots are built to run down after about six hours, and everything returns to normal. But because the person experiencing the trip is fully aware of the effect and not at all impaired in functioning, there can be a lasting impact, the way a peak experience impresses itself on you and becomes a kind of touchstone in your life."

"Oh, God." Dina looked stricken. "Do you mean…"

"Yes," said Nick. "Those white cross pills and saccharine tablets are what you said—people blowing the reporters off with something they knew wasn't C. But the ones that seemed to contain nothing at all were just sugar pills acting as carriers for Clarity nanobots. The 'Sixty Minutes' chemists couldn't detect them because they were too small and didn't correspond to any known chemical compound. But Clarity is real." He looked from Gabe to Dina and back again. "You felt it, and you felt it, and I felt it too. Let's not forget that."

"I think we've entered a space warp, Captain," said Gabe, rubbing his high forehead. "Let's just pretend for a minute that I understand what you're saying and we have placed teeny-tiny robots in the brains of America's youth. In our own brains! How do you know this is safe? How do you know the little robots aren't going to get together in the medulla oblongata or someplace and say, 'Hey, Fellas, that was fun. Let's go back and really mess with their minds?'" He shook himself like a wet dog. "How do we know *anything*? What the hell am I doing here?"

"This is completely safe," said Nick. "Gary has tested it under all sorts of conditions. Because he knows what he's tracking, he's been able to measure how fast the nanobots disperse, and whether they leave any trace. He's the smartest person I know, and I've seen his results. I'd trust him with my life: I did trust him with it, I was one of the people who took Clarity first."

"Yeah," said Dina, "you trusted him with my life too, you schmuck. So if this is so wonderful and harmless, why didn't you tell me?"

"You want the honest answer?" Nick looked sheepish, the choirboy overtaking the roué.

"No, man," said Gabe, shaking his dreads. "She wants you to lie to her."

Nick looked at Dina's lovely face, the wide cheekbones, the full mouth, the liquid brown eyes, knowing what he said could make her turn toward him or turn away. "The honest answer is that the minute I saw you at my door, I knew that I would move heaven and earth to do whatever you wanted, because I needed a second chance with you more than anything I could imagine."

"Be still my heart," said Gabe. "Wait till I tell Lance about this."

They both looked daggers at him. "Sorry," he said, "When I say I'll tell him about *this* I don't mean the fantastic nanobot voyage etcetera. Just that part about moving heaven and earth. I promise."

"Now you tell me, Dina," said Nick. "If I had laid out all these charts and explanations, would you have gone ahead?"

Dina stared at the ceiling above Nick's head. Sometime during Nick's show-and-tell, Alice the cat had jumped into her lap. Stroking Alice's silky fur, she silently shook her head no.

The only sound in the room was a loud, steady purr, but all of them were too busy with their own thoughts to hear it.

CHAPTER 7

❁

Dina didn't know what to feel. Everything was slightly unreal. The colors and shapes around her looked a little pixilated. Cradling Alice in her arms, she moved like a sleepwalker into the living room and sank into a beat-up leather armchair, inhaling its smoking-room scent. She resented Nick for manipulating her and hated herself for letting him. Yet it was true—Clarity seemed to be working until "Sixty Minutes" threatened to derail it, and if they dealt with that little glitch it would probably keep right on working. But she couldn't summon the energy to face it just then. She wished she could sit forever, dragging her fingers through Alice's fur, satisfied with the immediate feedback of a purr. She didn't want to look up at Nick. She dreaded looking at Gabe too, not wanting to confirm her fear that he hated her for involving him in this fiasco.

Nick crossed the room and settled onto the overstuffed arm of Dina's chair. Gingerly, he put his hand on the back of her neck. He felt her shiver, then hold herself very still.

Nick's hand was electric. Dina felt the energy penetrate her flesh, touching her deep inside, sending a buzz along her thighs, driving away her lethargy. She did not want a man who could deceive her this way to have so much power to affect her. Yet she didn't want him to let go.

When Nick spoke, it was as if he had read Dina's thoughts. "I didn't lie to you, Dina. Think about it. I never said Clarity was a chemical. We never discussed its composition at all."

Dina opened her mouth to protest, but Gabe, lying on the couch, beat her to it. "I got an A in catechism," he said. "They call that casuistry, or as my philosophy professor put it, 'Jesuitical truth.'"

Nick lifted both hands, surrendering. "Okay, you two. Let's call the whole thing off."

"No," said Dina, sitting up straight, suddenly determined. "But we've got to release this information, or we lose all credibility. I mean, look how suggestible people are. Look how suggestible *we* are. God! All of us took Clarity and had these profound experiences, and then Mike Wallace says it's speed and bim-bam-boom, Gabe and I start to question ourselves! If we don't put something out right away, that will be the end of Clarity. And if this one tanks, I for one am fresh out of ideas for working through the system."

"Amen to that," said Gabe, silently adding a prayer that the system didn't get its hooks into him for breaking its rules.

"Wait a second. That's not so easy," Nick told them. "Gary hasn't been sitting up in Alaska carving nanobots out of walrus tusks. He got this stuff the old-fashioned way: by hacking into computers at places like Zyvex and the Institute for Molecular Manufacturing and university departments and diddling around with their prototypes. We can't say anything about how we got it or how we made it, or we put him in jeopardy."

"Whoa there!" said Gabe, sitting up, his palms outstretched to halt Nick's stream of words. "What kind of jeopardy? Dina, you said this guy was the master of data encryption, that no one could ever track us. So how come he's vulnerable? And how come we're not? Not that I care if the entire military-industrial complex is onto us, you understand. I'm ready for the bamboo slivers, comrades. Just idle curiosity." A picture of Wilson popped into Gabe's mind, prison denims buttoned neatly to the neck.

"It's a different problem, man," Nick explained. "The Vitamin See press releases can only be traced to a fictitious e-mail address, a dead end, like sending people to a street address that turns out to be a vacant lot. But Gary didn't hack into these sites by e-mail. He took pains to cover his tracks, but if they have help from other expert hackers, they may be able to find evidence of communication between his computer and the nanotech companies. If we put anything out that mentions hacking in, they'll do their best to get up his ass in a nanosecond. We can say how Clarity works, but we definitely can't say how it was made."

"Fine," Dina said, abruptly businesslike. Her features rearranged themselves into a very different configuration: mouth set, eyes wide open—even the wild tangles of her hair seemed to snap to order. "We just cobble together a press release that's a summary of what you told us tonight—the science behind Clarity. No mention of hacking. It's anonymous, from 'Vitamin See,' with no traceable address, just like the others. They can take it or leave it."

Gabe felt so beat, he didn't really have the heart for more that night. Sighing, he thought about putting his head on Lance's shoulder. He had

Clarity to thank for Lance, no small thing. Still nursing his fears, he surrendered, leaving it to Dina and Nick to hammer out the press release.

They settled at the dining room table amidst Nick's charts and articles. He pulled a joint out of his pocket, raising his eyebrows inquiringly at Dina.

"I thought you never did that while you were working," she said.

Nick glanced at his watch. "It's 11:37," he said. "Does this still count as work? I thought it might lubricate any rough edges."

In the end, they smoked and struggled through their giggles for the correct tone of unattributed authoritativeness. It was hard to avoid self-parody, but by one a.m. they had a serviceable press release. Nick stood behind Dina, his hands on her shoulders, peering at the screen of her laptop for one final read-through. Dina tried not to feel the warmth spreading through his hands along her neck, her breasts, the length of her arms. At last he nodded. Ensuring the encryption software was set to protect her anonymity, Dina clicked *Send*.

Nick kissed the side of her neck, inhaling its fragrance of sun and flowers, something slightly tropical. He slipped a hand into her blouse.

Dina caught it with her own fingers. She clasped his hand to her breastbone like a shield. "Nick," she whispered, her nose buried in his arm, breathing his scent, "did you really mean it about wanting a second chance, about wanting it so much? Can I trust you this time? I don't think I can."

He spun her chair around, leaning in so they were almost nose-to-nose. "I meant it, Dina. I'm not pretending to be any less fucked-up than I am. I think you'd have to say that 'underachiever' was my middle name. I'm a defensive asshole. There are plenty of ways I'd like to have my life to live over. But what I said earlier was true. When I saw you again, I realized that I hadn't been able to draw a full breath since we split up. You and me, Dina, I just know it's supposed to be that way. That's what I want. You can trust that. But if you tell me its too late, that it can't happen, I'll go quietly."

Dina shook her head no, and Nick leaned all the way in, pressing his lips to her cheek, her chin, and just when she thought it would be impossible to wait an instant longer, her mouth. He wrapped his arms around her waist and pulled her to the carpet, their bodies pressed together, her legs opening to draw him in.

"O-o-owl," said Alice.

"O-o-owl," said Dina and Nick, in one voice.

❦   ❦   ❦

The press release created an instant furor. On the radio, Rush Limbaugh was rabid, unsure of whether to blame Fidel Castro or gays or "feminazis" for this heinous scheme to pollute the blood of young Americans with horrifying devices that might turn us into something out of the *Invasion of the Body-Snatchers*. Some treated Clarity like a health hazard, even though no incidents of harm had been reported. In southern California, for instance, some schools brought in psychologists to reassure children who might be traumatized by the idea of nanobots. But the therapists didn't have a firm grasp on the way Clarity worked, so often their interventions had an effect opposite from that intended, frightening children with terrifying analogies about little monsters living in their brains. On the principle of not asking for trouble, most school authorities canceled the sessions.

New Age types were unsure how to respond: on the one hand, the thought of achieving clarity had appeal, and Clarity itself was evidently non-polluting and otherwise non-toxic; on the other, the idea of little machines getting inside one's body was creepy—it sounded dangerous, intrusive, sort of Big Brother–ish. Internet traffic approached gridlock as such fine points—the individual's right to remain confused, for instance—were debated by students and activists and civil libertarians. A few people even tried to start Internet petitions condemning Clarity. But so many clear heads wrote to say that Internet petitions were a waste of time—especially those attached to no specific recipient, no actual legislation or public action—that for once they were withdrawn. Nick considered this a very good sign.

In fact, after an initial flurry, the Clarity controversy settled into a familiar polarity: Limbaugh and his ilk on one side, Vitamin See and its outright supporters on the other. Political and commercial opportunities were seized by those so inclined, while most people went about their business without giving the controversy too much thought.

In Congress, Texas Representative Tom DeLay was first out of the box to call for legislation against ingestible nanotechnology. He wanted to wedge the whole category onto Schedule One of the Controlled Substances Act, arguing that was the quickest way to give law enforcement officials the authority to stop anyone who tried to deploy this new technology. But some Big Pharma companies were heavily invested in nanomedical research, and DeLay's bill would put them out of that business, so Orrin Hatch—the drug companies' greediest campaign beneficiary—stood up in the Senate to counsel caution in the name of pure science, and the bill was stalled in committee.

A security company in New York made a small fortune overnight by offering "nanofilters"—devices that attached to air and water filtration systems, guaranteed to screen out any and all nanobots. That this guarantee was unenforceable had no effect on sales. Even if the filters had been fine enough to do the job, they couldn't control what leaked in through cracks in windows or open doors.

Such reactions made the three conspirators laugh: all that panic over the prospect of being made to see through lies? It was even rumored that certain officials and executives had hired food tasters to ensure they avoided consuming nanobots nesting in their steaks and baked potatoes. But how would the big shots tell if a dish was infested? The only test Gabe said he could imagine was waiting to see whether the food taster stood up from the table yelling, "Take this job and shove it!"

In short, while op-eds dueled and guardians of the public safety threw up their hands, there were outbreaks of Clarity everywhere. Auto dealers reported a glut of used SUVs on the market and a remarkable downturn in the demand for new models. In Oakland, California, a new youth organization had formed. The leader, Curtis Jackson, was a former crack dealer who decided after taking Clarity to find a new line of work. "I just looked in the mirror," he told the Sunday *New York Times* magazine, "and said 'How messed-up do you have to be to poison your own people so they keep filling this country's jails? Think what you could be doing with that energy!' So I did." The chairman of the Southern Baptist Convention came out in favor of gay marriage in the church, and no more than a week later, the president of the Orthodox Union did the same.

The loose activist coalition that had led anti-globalization demonstrations in Seattle and Montreal came to a consensus, denouncing blocking traffic as a misguided political strategy. "It doesn't take a genius to see we were generating more opposition in the name of creating empathy," one spokesperson said. "We're starting a process that will get people to hammer out a real program. This issue is too important to kid ourselves that we're doing anything about it merely by expressing our outrage."

Most remarkable was a mass desertion of Republican members of Congress from President Bush's scheme to reduce taxes on the rich. Gabe had heard through the grapevine that it was Dick Cheney's gay daughter who somehow introduced Clarity to an intern in the VP's office—who happened to be dating a Democratic Congress member's intern—and from there it made its way through the ranks of Congressional aides, more or less as a dare. Clarity-infused Democratic aide #1 to colleague: "What are you afraid of? I thought you were here for truth and justice." Colleague: "I am! Give it to me!" Democratic aide #2 to Republican counterpart: "What are you afraid of? If you really see the world the way your guy does, if you really believe all that trickle-up stuff, you've got nothing to lose. If it's true, it'll still be true. Or are you scared it isn't true?" Republican aide: "Of course not. Give it to me!" Etcetera.

The first member of Congress to break ranks was a cheerful-looking Republican from Ohio, Steve LaTourette, who must have been inclined toward skepticism about Bush's plan anyway: in 1998 he'd conducted a poll which revealed that 73.6% of his current constituents wanted the tax code abolished. Like all of his colleagues, LaTourette made no mention of Clarity when he introduced the press conference heralding the Republican opposition to the tax cut. But Gabe said he was certain—"I could be wrong, mind you, but, you know…I'm not"—based on LaTourette's open smile and choice of words.

"It's really pretty self-evident," the Congressman had said, "when you look at the numbers. The richest one percent own more of our nation's wealth than the bottom ninety percent put together, yet this tax cut gives them most of the benefit." He shrugged. "So you see, we really had no other choice."

"The truth," Gabe shouted at the TV set, "shall set you free!"

❦   ❦   ❦

While Gabe, Nick and Dina monitored the media, Clarity manifestations too local to register on the national news radar sprang up like dust devils. No one knew quite what to make of them.

In Calhoun County, South Carolina, there was a mass walkout of students at a white-flight "Christian academy" created by parents who couldn't abide sending their children to integrated public schools. Although the Supreme Court had issued its Brown vs. Board of Education decision in 1954, and President Eisenhower had sent National Guard troops to Little Rock in 1957 to enforce it, whites in parts of the deep South resisted integration for decades. In this central South Carolina county, when the desegregation order was finally implemented in the early Seventies, the public swimming pool was filled with cement and the one and only local movie theater closed its doors. From force of habit, the older generation of white parents called the public schools the "black schools," except when they talked to out-of-towners, and then it tended to come out anyway: "The bl…I mean the *public* school."

Christian academies were the crappiest of crappy schools, and the students knew it. In fact, the brightest Calhoun students discussed it at length at the end of almost every school day, hanging down by the creek on nice days and in Nicole's basement when it rained.

"I'm blazed," said Ashley, lying back on the lumpy couch, her head dangling off the seat, so that her strawberry blonde hair brushed the black-and-white checkerboard linoleum.

"Sort of," said Nicole, spread-eagled on the throw rug. "But this ain't bud. This ain't X. I don't feel all woo-woo. I'm still right here in the basement, looking at your upside-down face."

"Could you believe Miss Summers today?" asked Ashley, laying it on thick: "'*Outside agitators were the main cause of the "War Between The States.'*'" God! We are going to be flat-out ignorant when this place gets through with us."

"What a rinky-tink, mad fix we're in, Ash. I could hardly keep my face straight in science class. '*There is no way that the Earth could be over 10,000 years old.*' And when Ryan said did Mr. Burke believe that just because a preacher had said it, he said the evolutionists believe their theory just because some scientists said it!"

Ashley sat up straight. "So what is this about, Nic? Why are they doing this to us?"

"I read in a book that it was all about sex."

Ashley giggled. "You would. So how is it all about sex?"

"Well," said Nicole, "have you noticed how black and white can be together before a certain age or after a certain age? Like a baby can be with all colors, and the really old people don't seem to mind sitting next to each other on the porch at the senior center?"

"Hmm. I guess."

"Well, the guy who wrote this book said that the whole racial thing was about sex, that it was the people who were of an age to have babies that couldn't be together."

"I'll say!" exclaimed Ashley. "Remember when Brittany's mom found out about her and Darnell? That was brutal!"

"It's like don't even bother going there. But is that what it comes down to? They're so afraid of that, it makes them want to blow off our entire education? I'm wonder if we're even going to get into Midlands Tech. Does what we get even count as a real high school diploma?"

"Fuck this!" Ashley yelled. "Why are we just going along with this? We don't have to let them do this to us. Look, I'll call Brittany and you call Ryan and Kyle. I'll call Jordan too. And get Patty. Tell them to meet us here tomorrow, right after school. No smoke 'cause this is serious, but if Kyle has more C, that would be good."

Jordan had a cousin who worked at a radio station in Columbia, and she helped them figure out how to call a press conference. They called it for the site of the old movie theater. It wasn't that much of a drive from Columbia. Responding to encouragement from Jordan's cousin, who assured them of a real news hook, there was a local TV reporter and cameraman, and also a couple of other reporters with notebooks.

Ashley read their statement. "To keep us from sitting next to black kids, our parents have deprived us of good schools, up-to-date text books, art and music and language classes, a decent science program and even sports. They even closed this movie theater. If we didn't know better, we'd think the goal was to keep us ignorant and unprepared for college. We're all transferring to the public high school."

The cameras followed them into the registrar's office at the public school, just a couple of blocks away. Nicole's parents had a cow when they saw the six o'clock news, but she held her ground: she'd be eighteen before the school year was up and then she could do what she wanted anyway. Or did they want to get in the middle of some kind of campaign? "Free Nicole" messages on the Internet? After a tense, silent dinner, Ashley's folks came over and all four parents shut themselves into the kitchen for an hour. The dads came out red-faced and close-mouthed, and nobody tried to stop the girls when they set off for their new school the next morning.

❦   ❦   ❦

Back in California's capitol, no one had heard a whisper of the doings in Calhoun County. People's hands were full with trouble closer to home. The governor called a meeting to discuss the problem. "This is the God-damnedest thing," declared Hal Crayton, pounding the polished conference table for emphasis. "I don't know if I believe a word of it, but the Feds are making noises like it's time for an all-out alert, and we can't sit around with our thumbs up our asses, if you excuse the expression."

"I don't think they're saying these things can enter the body rectally," said Bob Bornstein, secretary of the Technology, Trade and Commerce Agency, the closest thing Hal Crayton had to a science advisor.

"Oh, is that your professional opinion, Bob?" The governor's tan had an intense burgundy undertone that clashed with the dusty blue velvet drapes. He didn't like wild cards, and this was one of the wildest. He looked down the length of the table. "So what proof do we have that these Clarity things are working?" he asked. "Dina, what's the scoop?"

Dina put a lot of her energy into making her face appear normal. Afraid her thoughts could somehow be read, whenever she found herself tempted to look directly at Gabe, she stared at an expanse of carpet embossed with the gubernatorial seal. "Well, sir," she said, "it's kind of ironic. All the symptoms so far point to increased intellectual curiosity and civic activism. There's been a huge push behind the Declaration of Interdependence Initiative; I think they've qualified for the ballot already, and the polls say it will definitely pass. And the Academic Senate at San Francisco State has come out with a resolution applauding students' call for longer classes to allow time for meaningful participation…"

There was uncomfortable laughter along the table.

"There's also been quite a bit of disruption of normal newsgathering processes, sir." She cleared her throat. "As you know from your last press conference." Barbara Hill had evidently been mixing it up with journalism students, because instead of blushing coquettishly when the governor complimented her hat and quietly resuming her seat when he ignored her follow-up questions, Barb had protested in a loud, clear voice, pinning Crayton to the wall with her well-documented queries about prison expenditures. When the governor had cast about for a softball questioner to save him, he'd had a hard time locating a familiarly somnolent face in the crowd. He'd never seen so many members of the press corps looking quite so alarmingly wide awake, and it scared the shit out of him.

The governor turned to the head of the Department of Alcohol and Drug Programs, Kathy Nakano, whose strong suit was crime prevention programs— all kinds of educational initiatives, neighborhood watch groups, things like that. "Kathy? What do we do here while the Feds talk tough? Is there some kind of information we need to be getting out there about people protecting themselves? Is there an interdiction plan?"

Kathy was a no-nonsense bureaucrat, a fairly rare breed. She fingered her trademark white neck bow as she talked. "I don't see the point of sugarcoating it, Governor," she said. "If this thing is real, what are we going to tell people? 'Don't swallow'? 'Don't breathe'? If the DEA comes up with some response to this, then we'll have to jump on the bandwagon. But right now, all we have is a legal substance that is being distributed free-of-charge. Even forgetting the Fourth Amendment stuff for a minute, I don't think we can justify asking local police departments to spend their resources on that, and if we put the Highway Patrol on it, what are they going to do? Right now, catching someone with Clarity is no more illegal than catching them with a glass of milk. We're having trouble finding the resources to deal with real crime out there. We'll look like fools if we divert troops to something that is basically pointless right now. I think it's better to do nothing than to take some action we have no way of evaluating. We'll just alarm people further, and I can't say it will do any good. Now if legislation is passed, that's another question. But I don't know that we want California to lead the pack there either, because enforcement costs money we haven't got right now."

"Gabe," said Crayton, looking grim.

Gabe started, then settled himself down, imitating calm. Today's Hawaiian shirt was positively understated: a vertical stripe made of some sort of trailing vine, green leaves on a pale blue background. "Yes, Governor?"

"Give it to me straight, Gabe. What are people saying about this thing?" The governor rubbed his forehead, then waved his hand in the air, like a man swatting flies. "Nano-fucking-bots," he muttered, "excuse my language."

"About what you'd think, Governor." Gabe shuffled his papers, as if he were searching for something. "The lunatic right is treating it like a communist conspiracy, the lunatic left is treating it like a government plot, and everybody in between is somewhere on a bell curve of moral panic. The thing is, the biggest part of the bell seems to be people who've tried this thing and are saying it makes them see clearly. No rumors of poison or bad trips so far. And you can imagine the alternative press and Internet sites are making hay out of how scared corporate America is that they might accidentally ingest something that made them see truth. There's a lot of Internet speculation about government crackdowns, but based on what Kathy is saying, I'd guess it's mostly paranoia so far." Gabe shrugged and shook his head as if this were the most uncanny thing. "So I guess I agree with Kathy. Sit tight. Check in again in a few days."

❀   ❀   ❀

"Whew!" Leaning her head against the cushioned banquette, Dina surveyed the gloomy bar they thought would provide the best cover. The place had a smell of maraschino cherries and old bourbon that reminded her of Grandpa David. No one seemed to notice them. She sipped her martini. "I'd have to say you win the Academy Award for best performance in a cabinet meeting."

"I owe it all to my supporting cast," said Gabe, gesturing gracefully toward Dina and Nick, as if strewing rose petals.

Nick seemed to be more or less living at Dina's place this week. The news was breaking so fast, there was always something to talk about, it just seemed easier this way. Besides, they were both finding it tremendous fun to play house: curl up in front of the TV to watch the news, carry their coffee into the bedroom of a morning, make love when the impulse took them. Even Alice seemed full of her old energy, racing down the hallway until they heard her claws skidding along the floor.

"But seriously," said Dina.

Gabe drew his hand down his face, changing its expression from giddy to grave, all ears. Nick broke into laughter, almost choking on his olive.

"But seriously," Dina repeated in a tone that brooked no opposition. "I don't think I can keep this up much longer. What if the DEA comes up with some emergency program and the states are supposed to comply? I can't sit there all day crafting lies for the governor to parrot, then spend all night strategizing the Clarity campaign."

"You can't do it because it's hypocritical," asked Nick, "or because you might blow your cover?"

Dina tried not to feel the pinch of that. Had it been hypocritical to help Crayton avoid being skewered for his education budget cuts? Probably. So what made this different? "Both," she admitted, "but to be fair, I've been hypocritical before. It just bothers me a lot more now."

"That's the Clarity talking," said Gabe. "Just wait till it wears off and I'm sure everything will fade back to a nice shade of gray." His tone was light, but Dina looked hurt. "I'm sorry, honey," he said. "I know you'll find this hard to believe, but I can't always remember to think before I open my mouth."

"No," she said. "You're right, I can't deny it. I just don't know what to do about it."

"Well, I realize this might be a radical suggestion, and maybe you just won't be able to take it seriously, but hey, Dina, what about all that leave you have saved up? Perhaps you could, you know, take a few weeks off the top. What do you think?" Gabe raised his emphatic eyebrows, miming polite curiosity.

"What's this?" Nick asked, blue eyes wide. "Is he serious?"

Dina blushed and nodded, caught out. "I'm just very busy and I didn't really have anyplace I wanted to go and, well," she swallowed, "I have about three years' worth of vacation time coming, if the statute of limitations hasn't run out."

Nick rubbed his hands together, smiling to show the dimples Dina's mother had so admired. "So what, that's like two months? More? How soon can you go?" he asked.

Once she made up her mind, it was easy for Dina to arrange to take her leave. The governor protested that this was a complicated moment to do without her, what with this nano-thing unfolding. But Dina pointed out that any other time she might have chosen would have been equally complicated for some other reason, which is why she'd never taken the leave that was coming to her, and since the governor could only serve two terms, she had just a few months left to do it. In the end, Crayton agreed this was probably her best opening.

❦   ❦   ❦

Nick's home in the Sonoma hills was nothing like the old Stinson Beach place. The splendid artisanship of the house was haute couture in comparison to the old house's off-the-rack ordinariness. And the setting was day to Stinson's night. Instead of the coast's salt tang and midnight chill, by June the hot inland sun had already begun to bake the green out of the grass, clouding the afternoon air with its sweet hay scent. On her walks, Dina gathered poppy, iris, and lupine. Now the house was filled with wildflowers—little bouquets in various stages of wilting crammed into jam jars and shot glasses on every table and shelf.

"This looks like a science fair experiment," Nick said. They sat on the couch, gazing out the window, silence broken only by the high electric buzz of insects. "We should be measuring something: how long it takes for the petals of iris to curl back on themselves, or for poppy pollen to drop."

"We are measuring something, but I don't know how to say it." Dina found herself beating back a sour mood. "How long before our little scheme is absorbed by commerce?" She pointed to yesterday's *Chronicle* lying on the couch. "Look at this fucking ad, will you! 'Herbal Clarity!' How long did that take? Look at the fucking DeLay bill! How long before Clarity is actually put onto Schedule One and people start getting busted? Is this what we wanted?"

Nick stroked her hair. He felt good. His inner voice had been pretty subdued lately. Spending this time with Dina had been delicious. "What did Gandhi have to say about how people might respond when God did dare to appear?" he asked her. "Run screaming in the opposite direction?"

Dina stuck her tongue out at him. He leaned over and gave it a soft lick. Nerves snapped to attention all over her body, but she tried to ignore them.

"Seriously, Nick," she said. "When we imagined this, our focus was on Clarity's impact—how would the world change if people woke up?" She punched the newspaper. "But all this is about fear and threat. The news is crammed with the reactions of people who are drumming up a moral panic. It's like Clarity is a security risk."

"You don't know how right you are," Nick replied. He tugged his laptop open and clicked on a bookmark in his Web browser. "I do this Google search every day, and every day there's more stuff that doesn't get written up in the papers. Look at this."

Dina had to admit she was impressed. The Declaration of Interdependence initiatives already had enough signatures to get on the ballot in twelve states, and there were only twenty-four initiative states in all. Because graduations were approaching, there had been a lot of activity about commencement speakers and ceremonies, mostly students rejecting the designated speakers in favor of their own more critical and thought-provoking choices. In Arkansas, a high school class valedictorian had been made to submit her speech to the principal for vetting, and the rejected text was now circulating doubletime in cyberspace. It was called "Who's Afraid of the Big, Bad Truth?" Dina peered over Nick's shoulder to read the first screen:

> Last week, I spent an extra hour after class with my biology teacher, trying to learn about the way aging affects the human brain. My teacher convinced me that most of the people who are in powerful positions, like lawmakers, probably still have all of their brain functions intact. If that is true, then I just don't get it! Old people seem to think that young people are stupid. They think that none of us will notice the huge fuss they are making over Clarity right now, or if we do notice it, we will believe what they say about doing it for our own good. But that is crazy! Here's how it looks to us: adults are going nuts and passing all sorts of laws because they're afraid of seeing things clearly. Period. And the fact that they don't think we will notice that this is what they're doing is proof of how dense they are!
>
> It's our turn to remake the world, to create the future. Old people are making much ado about nothing when it comes to Clarity corrupting young people. Even if they succeed in taking it away, they will fail, because we've seen through their lies, and we won't believe them again.

"She has a point," said Nick.

"What? That old people are stupid? I think I may qualify."

"No," he said. "You and I are sitting here reading the newspaper and treating it as the authoritative version of reality. This effort to put a lid on Clarity, I guess that's one side of the story. But there is another side—this mass of stuff on the Internet. Look, we know just about everything there is about media bias and media indifference to anything but the official story, right?"

Dina nodded.

"So why are we believing them now when they tell us the crackdown is the big story? What if it's a case of 'Pay no attention to the man behind the curtain'? What if this high-school girl and all the rest of what's happening that isn't making the newspapers is really the big story, and the crackdown is just a little background noise?"

"What if?" said Dina, resting her head on his shoulder to watch the Web pages click by. She tucked her hand under her arm and crossed her fingers.

❧   ❧   ❧

Dina phoned Nancy once or twice a week to check in. She and Gabe were taking turns feeding Alice and looking after Dina's place (which basically meant making sure no squatters had moved in, as Dina had long since killed all her houseplants with neglect). Clarity was a big conversation topic, even though Nancy still had no inkling of Dina's actual involvement.

"Have you seen this stuff that's floating around that says Clarity is a product of the international Jewish conspiracy?" Nancy asked. "One of my kids brought some of it into class today. God, it's so depressing. Let me read you this: 'In Japan they are already experimenting with jacks from computers directly into human brains, not to mention things like digital angel and their implantation of chips into people. If you do not think the Zionist community is controlling the media you watch then you need to research it, they are everywhere.'"

"Nice of them to call it the Zionist 'community.'" Dina laughed bitterly. "So warm and cuddly." She'd never been to Israel, and to her, the whole Mideast thing seemed like an intractable, incomprehensible nightmare. But she knew enough to spot when "Zionist" was being used as a synonym for "Jew."

"Yes," said Nancy. "So friendly and liberal. But some of my kids have been in the U.S. for just a few years, and they have no contact with actual-existing Jews. So they don't know how to interpret this garbage. One very sweet student from India said, 'My neighbor tells me the Jews started the Gulf War. Is that right?' After I answered him, he asked me another question."

"When did you stop eating Christians for lunch?"

"Nope. He wanted to know if Jews *were* Christians. And nobody laughed except me."

Dina wondered how Clarity's effect of seeing through illusions would play in a society that thought the material world itself was an illusion. She guessed the answer might come one of these days, but right now, there were limits to what one lab could produce. Nick said millions of tabs had been sent out through the network. He'd made up address labels for a funky fake mail order used-CD business, and he was sending jiffy bags out through six different post offices, just to avoid attracting too much attention. Distribution was focusing on the USA, obviously, and except for some activity in Canada, C didn't seem to be leaking much beyond its borders. Gabe said it was early for that, that X had taken years to spread around the world.

"So much for the global village," Dina said, commenting simultaneously on her inner and outer conversations.

"Maybe so," said Nancy. "I can't claim to know all that much about my Indian student's world, either. What are Jains, anyway? He kept talking about Dalit people, and I had to go look it up: those are the folks we were in the politically incorrect habit of referring to as 'untouchables.'"

"So what else have you been hearing about Clarity?" Dina asked.

"Well, there's major buzz about how it relates to *The Matrix*."

"The Keanu Reeves movie?"

"More like the Keanu Reeves cult." Nancy laughed. "I've got students who've seen it twenty times. There's a whole online Matrix-world. People are saying that Clarity was the catalyst for Keanu waking up in that scene where he suddenly sits up, bald as an egg, realizing that he's in an endless rank of bathtubs, plugged into a bunch of sockets. Someone sent me to a Web site that lays it all out—how the people behind *The Matrix* are the same ones behind Clarity. I have to admit it's semi-plausible, that the same people would use multiple ways of making their point: a movie, a drug, etcetera. I've got this quote from the filmmaker—let me read you a little bit now, and I'll e-mail you the link so you can catch the rest of it."

Nancy found the right bookmark in her Web browser and her computer screen filled with text:

> "The main idea in this movie, Larry Wachowski says, has less to do with the nature of reality than with what we make of our own realities. 'The Matrix is one of those things that just keeps going and going, an onion, layer after layer after layer. The Matrix is basically a system of thinking. This world has the Matrix all over the place—people accept ways of thinking that are imposed upon them rather than working them out themselves. The free-thinking people are those who question every sort of Matrix, every system of thought, be it political, religious, philosophical.'"

"So this means what? Dina asked. "Clarity is basically a marketing scheme for a movie? Like free *Star Wars* T-shirts?" She was impressed anew by how much faith people put in capitalism as the engine of creativity.

"No, Dina. You're not getting it. They don't see *The Matrix* as a product. It's like a bible to them, or an arcane metaphysical allegory that just happened to get delivered as a movie. You know, it's a very ancient idea: the real world is illusion, *maya*, and only the superior being is able to awaken to a higher, immaterial reality."

"So what you're saying is they've found a way to understand Clarity—which is supposed to be about eliminating false consciousness—as something that gives them elite status based on associating it with a character in a movie?"

"Big deal," laughed Nancy. "You sound like you own stock in the company. Kids have a million ideas—God, I believed every conspiracy theory I heard when I was their age. What's it to you?"

Too close for comfort, Dina thought. She dissembled, changing the subject to Alice's care and feeding, then said goodbye. But after she'd hung up, she found the conversation had upset her. She and Nick sat on the couch with his laptop resting on their legs while they checked out the Web site Nancy mentioned.

"Fuck it," said Dina, staring past the smooth wooden curves of the house to the dust-dry grass outside. "I should just collect my booby prize for major hubris and throw in the towel. You asked if God did dare appear, would people run screaming the other way? But what made me think people's reaction wouldn't be to start marketing God coffee mugs and trying to book God for celebrity endorsements?"

"Whoa, wait up!" Nick looked amused.

Dina saw flashes of that cute condescension that always pushed her buttons, but she decided not to say anything. He'd been so sweet.

"The most anything can be is a tool," Nick continued, a little pedantically. In this light, lecturing, he reminded her a little of Mr. Chips. "You can't control what people do with it. I remember Gary telling me that when we first got into the business. There was all this pot and acid in 'Nam, and he thought it would be incredible, that all the soldiers would trip and that would make them realize war was wrong and they'd put down their guns."

"There were a lot of desertions," said Dina, hopefully, laying her head on the sofa pillows, wedging her bare feet under Nick's leg.

"Yeah. But there were also lots of guys who couldn't believe how great mortar fire looked when you had taken a couple of hits of LSD. If any tool could control how it was used, that would be amazing. I remember this woman talking about how great she'd felt about not giving her kid toy guns, until she saw him running through the yard with a carrot, pointing it at his sister and yelling 'Pow!' You can make the tool, but you can't control how people use it."

"Even Clarity," said Dina, chewing on a hangnail.

"Even Clarity."

Go ahead, said Nick's inner voice, encouraging for a change. Dina had been giving him blessing lessons lately. It was actually a very clever thing. She explained that when people had a stubborn worry or a problem they couldn't lick, it was useless offering them advice. Q: *Have you tried this?* A: *Yeah, it did-n't work.* Q: *Well, how about this, then?* A: *No, that's no good....* You just get into that dumb tennis match where they bat back every idea you serve and you both end up feeling frustrated. The blessing idea was to give them some positive energy instead of unwanted advice.

Reaching his hands toward Dina's dark curls, Nick looked into her big brown eyes. "Dina, I bless you that all of the high purpose and effort you've put into Clarity comes back to you as delight in seeing people use this new tool for good, and doing that of their own free will."

Dina laughed, tickled.

"Amen," said Nick. "Remember, you've got to say 'Amen' to seal the blessing."

"Amen, amen," she said, sitting up and putting her arms around his smooth neck, inhaling his cool-water scent. "May it be so."

CHAPTER 8

Dina found it hard to go back to work at the end of her leave: Sacramento in August, the frying pan *and* the fire. The morning weather forecast warned of a high over 100 degrees. As she got ready to leave the house, Alice was o-o-ow-ling at top volume, at once happy to have her companion back and worried that Dina might again disappear for weeks, leaving her with no company beyond Gabe's or Nancy's quick visits at feeding time.

Walking to her car, Dina felt like owling herself. They were burning off fields in the valley, producing a quality of air that one didn't breathe so much as chew and swallow. The lawns were turning brown and all the trees had a dusty look. Hot air hovered over the blacktop, making things look wavy and unstable, an underwater prospect in a waterless world. At eight a.m., the temperature had already exceeded Dina's comfort zone. Her faint hope was that these same conditions meant the office would be sparsely populated for her return—that unlike herself, her coworkers had been smart enough to take their vacations when Sacramento was uninhabitable—so she wouldn't have to tell too many lies her first day back.

But who knew what to expect? The last couple of months, things had been harder than usual to predict. It was as if there had been a subtle shift in energy fields, some little click or hitch in the world's turning. Before her leave from the governor's office, Dina had understood that Clarity was perceived as a threat. In her professional sphere, the main focus of attention was on avoiding, preventing, and spinning it. But during her time away, she'd been able to view the situation from a different perspective. Now she found herself waiting for all the little changes to aggregate into something truly major, something too big to spin into nothing. She could feel it coming.

Shepherding Clarity had by no means been a full-time occupation. In many ways, her two months away were a true vacation, deliciously slow and satisfying. Dina and Nick stayed around Nick's place—she didn't want to be too far from Gabe and the computer in case of unforeseen events, and her reluctance prevailed over Nick's idea that they should spend the time on a tropical island. But she'd had a real rest. They slept late and made love in the morning light, took long walks in the brown hills and made lots of excursions into Healdsburg and Santa Rosa, into San Francisco for entertainment and shopping.

From her time in the land of real life (as opposed to the surreal world of electoral politics), Dina could see that certain things had undeniably changed. People tended to look you in the eye much more. Nick and Dina both found themselves in many more conversations with strangers—not just "Hello, how are you?"—growing out of casual encounters in theater and grocery lines, bookstores, restaurants. The first week of Dina's leave, they'd gone to the movies three times, a delightful treat. At each show, the audience booed and protested so loudly at the commercials for Coke and the U.S. Army screened before the main features, it had been impossible to hear. A phalanx of ushers had come down the aisles pleading for silence, but it wasn't granted until the feature began playing. By the last week of July, the commercials had disappeared, and movies were back to the pre-1990s standard fare of trailers and features.

At a big newsstand in the city, they'd bought specialist periodicals—*Advertising Week*, *Variety*, the *Industry Standard*, the *Wall Street Journal*, *Women's Wear Daily* and others. Nick pored over them, looking for clues. *Variety* reported surprisingly low grosses for action flicks. Both *Lara Croft, Tomb Raider* and the Vin Diesel epic *The Fast and the Furious* had flopped at the box office. Commentators wondered whether the studios had finally saturated the public's appetite for mindless violence. *Ad Week* noted that major advertisers—most of their "Superbrands," including McDonald's, the wireless phone companies, Toyota, Nissan, and Dodge—were reporting unprecedented levels of consumer complaints, more than quadruple the volume of twelve months previous. Every time a commercial ran on TV, calls and e-mails spiked. Some of them had to do with imagery—people offended by blatantly manipulative appeals to sex and the romance of individuality—while others focused on content, the gas-guzzling environmental irresponsibility of SUVs.

Overall, the *Journal* said, certain types of discretionary expenditure were down: Nike, Tommy Hilfiger, and other heavily promoted teen-market brands showed a marked dip in sales compared to a year before. There had been dozens of stories about stockholder revolts: small shareholders showing up at meetings armed with surprisingly thick dossiers on board member conflicts-of-interest and other corporate misdeeds; internal documents that had somehow been obtained and released to the press by corporate watchdogs. There had been a scandal story about a different company most every day.

"So other than busting corporate America, what are people doing with their lives," asked Dina, "if not going to slasher movies and buying $200 sneakers?"

Nick couldn't say precisely, but from the way things looked in Sonoma County, he thought the answer might be having more private and less commercial time. "Well, it's summer, I know, so you're bound to see lots of families, but I've never seen so many people on the trails at this point in the season. And I know this seems odd to say, but they seem more *present*. You know, everyone says hello and they notice you, instead of looking off to the side as you pass."

Dina had seen it too. At the farmers' market in Healdsburg, she'd felt this odd sensation, like one of those dreams where a familiar landscape turns into something quite strange. But there had been nothing ominous about it. To the contrary, it was the absence of pressure and menace that she'd noticed. Kids walked and talked in groups, but without the usual swagger. Shoppers questioned vendors, who answered patiently. Dina agreed with Nick; his choice of words made sense. She'd used the same ones herself: a heightened feeling of presence, an unexpected solidity in others' attention and, she supposed, in her own awareness.

❦   ❦   ❦

On the way upstairs to her office, silently hushing the butterflies in her stomach, Dina ran into Jeanette Woo. "Hot enough for you?" asked Jeanette, looking fresh in a white cotton blouse and an efficient ponytail.

"Yes, thank you." Dina fanned herself with one hand, leaning against the tiles lining the staircase. Mercifully, they still felt cool. "What a reentry back into Sacramento! I fooled myself into thinking it was warm enough in Healdsburg."

"Proving my theory that you should never leave this town. It just makes you soft."

"So what are you doing here at this ungodly hour?" Dina saw a cameraman lurking a few steps behind Jeanette and, off to one side, teams from other news outlets.

"Want the official answer or the truth?" Brushing black bangs off her forehead, Jeanette waited for a reply, exactly as if her question had been serious.

There's that reality shift again, thought Dina. Maybe Jeanette was serious. Dina decided to play along. "Uh…the truth, I guess."

"Press conference to cover up the incipient energy deregulation scandal. We've had the rolling blackouts and the skyrocketing bills, but I heard we haven't seen the end of it. Apparently, it's much larger than they're saying. So this is some kind of 'California Energy Plan' that's supposed to prevent more problems in future. But I think it's just a way to deflect attention from what's already happened." Jeanette's shrug implied business as usual.

But to Dina it seemed anything but usual. She was truly nonplussed. She and Jeanette had done the heads-up thing before, almost-friends exchanging courtesies, saving up goodwill for a rainy day—like when Jeanette had phoned her about the student editors before the governor's press conference. But Jeanette had never before stepped outside her Jean Arthur girl-reporter role: ironic, cynical, yet careful not to say anything that, if repeated, might offend the powers-that-be. Today, she sounded so sincere!

Jeanette stared at Dina, head cocked to one side, eyes wide. Dina, feeling the other woman could see her thoughts, hastened to tidy them up.

Jeanette laughed, a full, earthy sound. "Maybe you actually wanted the official answer after all," she said.

"No, no. I've been offered the truth many times in this building," Dina said, gesturing at the offices above her. "I guess I was just feeling a little stunned. I'd say this is the first time I actually got it. Thanks." She was almost sure Jeanette winked at her.

The first person Dina saw in the office was Elena, the aide whose boyfriend had a reconciliation with his brother under the influence of Clarity.

"Dina!" Elena seemed genuinely delighted to see her. "You look wonderful! Look at that tan! I guess being on leave agrees with you."

"Thanks. I guess it does. I feel pretty good, now that I'm in a totally air-conditioned atmosphere. So, did you all manage to keep it together without me?"

Elena was quiet, clearly thinking it over.

Following Elena's lead, Dina checked in with herself, noticing that she'd been expecting an immediate quip in response to her question. Typically, she would have accepted that as normal and sufficient: an exchange of formalized sounds that stood in for communication.

"Well, I don't think you should feel guilty about being away, if that's what you're asking," said Elena at last. "I'd say things are a little fractured here. The governor and some of the department heads are trying to control all this uppity attitude that's been surfacing out there, and everybody else is kind of going with the flow. But it isn't like you could have changed that, you know?"

Feeling like a hypocrite, Dina nodded her agreement. Hadn't she and Nick and Gabe helped to change it already, from the old way to this strange new world?

Elena lowered her voice. "Actually, I think it's pretty cool. Like people are waking up or something. Except around here." She motioned toward the governor's office. "As to what will happen, as my boyfriend says, '*El tiempo da buen consejo*'—time will tell."

Making it to Gabe's office, Dina shut the door and lowered a pile of file folders to the carpet, sinking into a chair in their place. She could barely see Gabe over the stacks of paper. He mumbled something into the phone, then put it down and rushed to greet Dina. "Before I say a word, I need to know something. Are you Gabe or a clever reproduction?" she asked.

Smiling, Gabe pinched himself. "Ow! Well, I guess I could be faking that, but it sure felt like I was getting pinched right then, so I'd take a wild guess and say yes, it's me." He stared at Dina. "And what, by the way, is motivating that question, Ms. I-look-ten-years-younger-from-being-in-the-country?"

Keeping her voice at a whisper, Dina mimed a big kiss and said, "Well, Jeanette Woo just told me the unvarnished truth without blinking an eye, and Elena seems to have matured about a decade, and I'd say there's just a slight wrinkle in the time-space continuum, or something. But maybe that's just reentry."

Gabe nodded, smoothing the front of his grass green shirt strewn with bright parrots. "All of the above, Captain. I'm sure the reentry thing must be giving you the bends, and yes, I'd say you were right about that wrinkle." He spread his arms wide. "Welcome to Schizopolis."

"As in schizophrenic?"

Gabe nodded. "There's some kind of generation gap going on around here, but it isn't really about age. Half the day I'm in meetings where the governor's senior people are getting all beside themselves over the dreadful news that the Dow is down and people aren't consuming as much high-priced shit as they used to and the whole corporate energy scam isn't going to pass by unnoticed—and I'm supposed to tell them what 'the street' is thinking, for Christ's sake!" Gabe shook his head like an agitated horse, sending his dreads flying. "And the other half I'm surfing the Internet and talking to friends and using my James Bond encryption software. Am I coming or going? And how long can I wait for the answer? Girlfriend, I am so glad you are back to save me from being alone with this thing."

"Me too, I guess. Although truth be told, I'd rather have stayed on vacation."

"I bet. So how was it living with the mysterious Nick for weeks at a time?" Gabe settled into an anticipatory grin, guessing what the answer might be.

Dina stretched suntanned arms above her curly head, yawning. "Delightful, delicious, de-lovely," she said. "It was like something out of a romance novel: walks on the beach, trips to the farmers' market, holding hands in the movies."

"Or out of a personal ad," said Gabe, unable to resist.

Dina threw a pencil at him. "Speaking of personal ads, how's Lance?"

Smiling, he lobbed the pencil back. "Just fabulous, thank you." Gabe raised his voice to finish the lyric: "'…it's delectable, it's delirious, it's dilemma, it's de limit, it's deluxe, it's de-lovely.'"

"So this little adventure of ours isn't a total loss."

"By no means, and if I gave that impression, I sincerely apologize to my constituents."

"Are you sorry you did it, Gabe? I guess what I'm asking is, are you sorry I involved you in all this stuff that requires deception?"

Gabe looked serious, mouth turning down and brow wrinkling as he thought it over. "Honestly, Dina, no," he said. He gestured over the mountain of papers toward his computer screen. "I guess I would have been happy to be an innocent bystander too. Just to be noticing all this stuff that's happening— the Declaration of Interdependence thing is on the ballot for sure, and people are saying there's a public campaign financing initiative brewing that could finally get the big money out of politics." Gabe clasped his hand to his chest. "Be still my heart! All these corporate scandals: I think we may have finally put a damper on the idea that corporations should be the model for all good things. People might even be ready to consider that the bad old public sector isn't the source of all evil. Just the feeling of things, the little stories and new Web sites and…I don't know, the texture of things. And me and Lance. I guess I'd be happy if all that was happening without my having had anything to do with it. But—call me crazy—I just feel a little bit better knowing I did. Y'know?"

"I know." Dina felt her cheeks flush with excitement. "Me too. And it hasn't even been five months since the launch. You said it would take six months to tell if it was going to work, but I think the verdict is already in, don't you?"

They were high-fiving each other when the governor's secretary came in to say it was time for the meeting.

❧   ❧   ❧

"Welcome back, Dina," said Hal Crayton at the head of the mahogany conference table, showing his pearly whites. "We missed you. But I must say, you don't look like you missed us. Nice time?"

"I had a wonderful time," she said brightly, sliding into her seat. "Thanks for asking."

Pleasantries out of the way, the governor got down to business. "Okay," he announced, "let's hear the damage for this week."

One by one, the department heads reported news—or at least buzz—in their areas. Kathy Nakano was characteristically brisk with her bulletin from the drug wars. "The DeLay Bill is still jammed up in committee. It seems some committee members are worried that adding nanotech to Schedule One is going to put the lid on medical research that looks pretty promising. They think it might tar the whole field and put us behind the other countries that are making advances."

"That your take too, Bob?" Crayton turned to hear from Technology, Trade and Commerce. Bornstein swallowed, looking like a deer in the headlights. "That's what I'm getting, Governor. The Silicon Valley boys are calling, talking up restraint of trade, interfering with the natural functioning of the market, all that. Much bigger than medical marijuana, they say."

Dina couldn't control herself. "Excuse me, Governor, but I'm afraid I didn't follow the news as closely as I should have while I was away."

"I'm sure you'll catch right up," he said.

"I'm sure I will. But from what I've been reading, this Clarity thing is tied to citizen action, not a crime wave. Couldn't this be good for the Democrats?"

"You *have* been gone awhile." This was Len Marietta, the governor's chief of staff. He had that sleek corporate look, like an anchorman: never a salt-and-pepper hair out of place, never a wrinkle in his suit. Dina got the feeling he coordinated his wardrobe with his environment; for these meetings, he always wore a blue that harmonized with the velvet drapes. "In the meantime," Len said, "they've invented a little thing called an election. You know, with campaign contributions. How many contributions are the Democrats going to get if they come out in favor of kids ingesting robots and storming corporate offices?"

"Storming?" Dina was genuinely amazed. "I don't think I read about that. What do you mean 'storming'?"

"If I may," said Gabe. "I've asked the folks in my network to help me do a roundup. Since April first, there've been forty-seven stockholder suits filed against corporate leadership, and in twenty-one of those cases, stockholder attempts to address board meetings. But no one has reported violence or arrests." He looked at Len. "Maybe my informants are missing something."

"Fine," snapped Marietta. "Forget storming. Let's just focus on forty-seven attempts to scare potential contributors shitless, forty-seven expensive lawsuits to defend. What was that we said about California's business climate? 'California is good for business.' My ass."

"What else, Gabe?" the governor asked. "Where is the street on this?"

"Depends which street you mean, Governor. Wall Street, not too happy. But you heard what Bob said about the hi-tech guys. Most of them are pretty clean when it comes to business ethics, it seems. Some of the senior people still believe what they used to say about freedom of thought and so on. Almost all the consumer lawsuits are against energy companies, auto companies, fast-food corporations, and over-the-counter pharmaceuticals. So I don't think we can say business is all on one side of the issue, but big finance, oil, and heavy industry are pretty unhappy. The constituency groups I deal with aren't complaining, though. This thing seems to be bringing them more members. The buzz I hear is that interest is at an all-time high. And there's an attention to strategic thinking that seems new. It feels like people aren't being so reactive—it isn't 'Let's all go protest this,' as much as 'Let's sit down and figure out how to handle this.' A candidate who could harness this energy could go far." *The kind of candidate you used to be*, Gabe thought, but forbore to say.

"Okay," said Ron Weiss, the governor's counsel, looking hugely annoyed. "I don't want this to sound any more like a campaign meeting than it already does. We aren't going to get caught using the governor's office to talk about contributions and campaign strategy, so let's change the subject."

Ron had to repeat that intervention several times before the meeting ended, and Dina had to bite her tongue almost until it bled. After work, she and Gabe had one of their double-martini suppers, but this time, the tone was different.

"So is this what Clarity is going to do for us, Gabe? We'll keep phoning it in at the governor's office and kvetching after hours. *Plus ça change, plus c'est le même chose?*"

"I could be wildly off base here, honey, but I think we both know the answer to that." Gabe tossed his head, his dreads making a little leap before settling into place again. He looked Dina in the eye, reaching into his bottomless well of soul tune lyrics to imitate Arthur Alexander: "You be-e-et-ter move on."

"*We* better move on," said Dina. "But it's not as if we even have a choice. What am I agonizing about? It's August now, the election's in November, and come January, somebody else will have the problem of choreographing the Honorable Hal Crayton's press conferences anyway. I'm going to try to see it through to the election, just to finish what I started. But, shit, Gabe, if I can't stick it, there's really no harm in leaving before that. I'm never going to want this kind of job again. Are you?"

Gabe thought it over. "Depends what you mean by 'this kind of job.' I don't think I'm going to want to do community organizing for a straight-up Democrat again—unless they put Clarity in the water at the Demo convention. But I don't think I'm ready to give it all up, everything I've learned. My

Rolodex!" He clasped an imaginary Rolodex to the bosom of his Hawaiian shirt. "I'd like to use these powers for good, if you catch my drift."

Dina nodded. They clicked glasses and ordered another.

❧   ❧   ❧

Meanwhile, the Cheney family was having a very unusual Sunday supper at daughter Mary's rustic home in the mountains outside Denver.

A year earlier, Mary had retired as Coors' gay/lesbian corporate relations manager—to avoid tainting her father's vice presidential campaign, it was said. Gabe knew her from the wonderful world of community outreach. One of her specialties had been softening up communities unlikely to welcome a gay-Coors alliance—such as Latinos—by sending in crack teams fully conversant in both cultures. Her politics were hardly identical with Gabe's; after all, Mary supported her father, which Gabe could never do, and she belonged to the school that thought out-groups could more easily win acceptance as markets than as movements, which was not Gabe's view. But their paths had crossed at conferences—the Human Rights Campaign, the National Gay & Lesbian Task Force—each of them recognizing the other's mastery of a particular terrain. Despite himself, Gabe liked her. She seemed brave in a sort of Katharine Hepburn-ish way, and Kate was his favorite.

The last time they'd met had been not long after the Mike Wallace piece on Clarity, when Vitamin See's nanotechnology press release had been issued. Over drinks in the hotel bar, a whole gang of conferees had wound up talking about Clarity as a stellar example of viral marketing. Gabe hung back, not wanting to show his hand; but he had been truly tickled by all the nice things people said about his media strategy, and especially intrigued to hear Mary's partner Helen ask if it wasn't illegal, why couldn't they try it?

Later, he'd slipped Helen a few tabs, saying he'd gotten them from a friend at the conference, swearing her to secrecy so his friend wouldn't get into trouble. She'd happily consented to keep his confidence, and she and Mary had a pretty interesting evening testing Clarity on themselves. What had become abundantly clear was that you could get a serious pain in the neck from holding a position halfway in the closet and halfway out.

They'd decided to share the news with Mom and Dad. August was a good time to be out of Washington and in the mountains, a time for family. The ostensible occasion was a long-postponed celebration of the publication of Mom's children's book, released in May. It was holding at number four in the picture book bestseller list, having risen to the top of the list in July.

The mountain air breezed through the open window, fresh now after a hot afternoon. The table was festive—bright napkins and placemats to complement the southwestern furniture and the vase of Mexican paper flowers that was Mary's habitual centerpiece. Everyone was relaxed after an afternoon ride, all freshly showered in jeans and comfortable shirts.

A decent interval after Dad's favorite gazpacho, Mary told her parents they'd imbibed Clarity along with the soup course. Dad had been apoplectic at first, sputtering, reaching for his cellphone to call…who?

"Dad," said Mary, donning her good-daughter blonde-ponytail expression and using the voice that usually pacified horses and dogs, "this can't hurt you. You aren't going to feel woozy or see strange things or get addicted or anything. I promise. You'll just be able to see things more clearly, to see more of what's there. How do you feel right now?"

"Normal, I guess." He had turned an alarming shade of maroon, but now the color began to subside. He looked at Lynne.

"Fine," she snapped, the narrow pink bow of her lips clenched tight. But she couldn't keep it in. She was horrified. "Mary, how could you? This is unforgivable! How could you dope your own parents?"

"Mom, Dad, calm down! Let me explain. This isn't dope, and it only has one impact, which is consistent with everything you've taught me—not to accept what others are saying just because they say it, but to look beneath the surface and decide for myself what's true."

"Well, now, that's right, Mary," said Lynne. "We did teach you and Elizabeth to thine own self be true." She looked at Dick, who seemed a little odd. "Isn't that right, Dick?"

Dick nodded like man in a trance.

"Dad! Are you okay?"

He nodded again.

"What are you thinking, Mr. Cheney?" Helen seldom addressed either Cheney parent directly. When Lynne first made it clear that Mary was expected for Thanksgiving—provided she came unescorted—Helen had gotten the message, even though it hurt. She kept quiet, thinking they might come around in time as they got to know her and see how happy Mary and she were together. But she just had to risk speaking up now: this was the first time she'd seen Mary's father at a loss for words. "Mr. Cheney," she called, in the tone of voice she'd use to reach the other end of a long hall. "Mr. Cheney!"

"Remember that *Post* story about Halliburton dealing with Iraq?" he asked, speaking much more slowly than usual.

Helen had no idea, but Lynne and Mary nodded.

"During the campaign, I told them that when I headed Halliburton, I had a firm policy against trading with Iraq, even though we did business with Iran and Libya. I told them I had no idea our subsidiaries were trading with Iraq. But I did. I authorized it because the company's bottom line was more important to me than the policy." Taking off his glasses, Dick massaged his nose where the eyepiece bit into his skin. "Is this what this damn stuff is supposed to make you do? Kick yourself in the ass for everything you've done?"

"Not necessarily, Daddy." Mary looked hard at her father. "But maybe for those things you truly regret."

"I'm afraid I'm going to regret that one," he said. "It wasn't such a great idea to do it and say we didn't." Dick chuckled bitterly. "I guess we taught you and Elizabeth that too, hmm?"

"And to stand up for yourself." Mary grabbed Helen's hand. "Right, Mom?"

"Yes, honey. Of course." Lynne looked a little confused.

"Then you'll understand, Mom, why I have to say this, because I've been thinking about it for a year." A tear trailed down Mary's strong nose. "When Cokie Roberts told you I was openly gay, why did you deny it?"

"I di….." Lynne's mouth trembled, putting an end to her reflexive denial. Suddenly, her brimming eyes spilled over, melting wet tracks into her makeup. She covered her face with her hands. "Because I was ashamed! And now I'm ashamed again—of myself. How could I do that to you, Mary? You're right, it's against everything we've ever taught. Can you ever forgive me?"

Mary took a deep breath. "I can forgive you if you never ever do it again. I love you two. But if you keep on making me feel like something that needs to be swept under the carpet, I won't be able to trust you. And I won't be able to go to bat in the next campaign." Under the table, Helen squeezed Mary's hand hard, three times, their signal for "I love you."

The floodgates had opened. They talked about everything until none of them had been able to stay awake any longer. Mary confided how hard it had been to serve as liaison to the gay market and maintain her loyalty to the party when Republicans said so many awful things about gays and lesbians. Dick disclosed how easy it had been to get carried away in the political moment and say whatever was expected of him. And how hard it was to serve without complaining under a man with a fraction of his experience and intellect. Lynn, now crying full out into her bright purple napkin, said that in political life, everything you said and did was vetted for its impact on votes and contributions, and that sometimes she wished she could return to her first love, poetry, leaving all this behind. Even Helen was able to share a little of the pain it had caused her to be rejected by the family of the most important person in her whole world.

The following day, Dick contacted his counsel, Mary Matalin, to say that the next time someone asked about Halliburton, she shouldn't respond with a denial unless she knew it to be true. He was scheduled for "Meet The Press" that Sunday, but at the last minute, Colin Powell went on as a substitute, mumbling something about an unavoidable scheduling conflict. No one could confirm the rumor that Dick was transported to an undisclosed location until an intensive course of post-Clarity reeducation could be administered. Nor could anyone explain precisely why Lynne was uncharacteristically quiet that summer. But it was verified by a reporter for *The Advocate* that Mary and Helen were planning a commitment ceremony in November, followed by a Hawaiian vacation.

❧   ❧   ❧

As the Clarity campaign picked up steam, the rumor mill began rolling faster. The co-conspirators met at Dina's for a summit on security, a reality check. A creaky fan nudged warm air around the living room. Nick and Dina sat together on the couch, while Gabe took the armchair. Ice cubes rattled as they sipped gin-and-tonics from sweating tumblers.

The Clarity campaign sometimes seemed like a bizarre psychological experiment, revealing surprising insights into the putative participants' mental processes. One interesting wrinkle had to do with the gap between many people's assessment of the might and vigilance of the powers-that-be versus the often inept actuality. For instance, the Internet was full of fearful speculation about crackdowns on Clarity. Gabe and Nick had each collected a raft of false reports that Clarity's originators had been traced and arrest was imminent. Others said that Clarity's creators had already been apprehended. This was from a Web site devoted to drug arcana:

> I met an old friend last night. He told me that his wife received a call from her cousin last week. The cousin lives out in the desert, near 29 Palms, and her husband does desk work at the local police department. It seems he was on the desk late one night last week when a big bust came down. They brought in half a dozen guys and all sorts of lab equipment, but the cousin said it was all very hush-hush, without the usual paperwork.
>
> After they hustled the prisoners out in an unmarked car, the cousin's husband had a quick look through the stuff that was stored in property. There were several

hundred boxes filled with bottles, and all the bottles were filled with white pills marked C. When he went back for another look last night, the boxes were gone.

Anyway, the info came to me by way of a long route. But the sources are "innocent bystanders" with no reason to lie. My friend swears the info is accurate, that he called back to get it first hand from the cousin, confirming what his wife said.

I thought this was worth passing along. Especially since Clarity is legal as far as I understand. There hasn't been a word in the news about any bust. I guess it seems the federal gov't doesn't have too much respect for the law or the truth—or the civil liberties of whoever got taken away in that unmarked car. But if the C supply dries up, now you know why.

Of course, each of the three principals reacted differently to these reports.

"According to the wild waves," said Gabe, using his new name for the World Wide Web, "we've all been busted and are being tortured until we reveal our sources and suppliers. Now, I don't feel a thing, but what do I know? Maybe it's some new form of painless torture. But seriously, the consensus is they're hunting us like public enemy number one," he cleared his throat, "and, well, I just wondered. Are they? I mean, should I be packing up food and water and heading for a cave someplace?"

"The rumors of my death are greatly exaggerated," Nick replied. "Mark Twain," he whispered to Dina, winking. "Listen, man, all I can tell you is that Gary is hypervigilant and he hasn't detected a single sign that our security has been compromised. He's examining his log files, searching regularly for setuid root files and setgid kmem files, checking his system binaries, looking for packet-sniffers, all kinds of unauthorized entries—the whole ball of wax."

"Packet-sniffers!" laughed Dina. "That sounds vaguely obscene."

"Well," said Gabe, "this is probably naïve, but you know, I'm just a little curious. Why the fuck not? Why *aren't* they coming after us?"

Dina shook her head. "What, you mean like they've gone after crack and eliminated it? Or heroin? Illegal immigration? Illegal arms sales? Need I go on? I have a name for this delusion," she told them. "The paradoxical rescue."

"Meaning what?" Nick looked a little interested and a little skeptical, a characteristic combination Dina was beginning to find endearing.

"Meaning even though we see evidence everywhere of the authorities' ineptitude, we just can't let go of the idea that they are a bunch of Supermen. Think about all those movies featuring government uber-agents using their ultra-hi-tech computers in underground labs to pinpoint incidents of wrongdoing and beam up the Tac Squad. I get why it works in the movies—got to have black hats and white hats. But we aren't actually living in sci-fi world. Look how long it takes them to get to the bottom of things, if they ever do: look at the Unabomber! He was cooking up his bombs and mailing manifestos and schlepping his explosive packages by Greyhound for ages before they got wind of him. They can't even interdict the drugs they've thrown untold millions of dollars at for decades. Plus Clarity isn't even illegal yet—Gabe, back me up, we sat right there in the governor's conference room and heard Kathy Nakano say there was nothing the police could do until it was, right?"

Gabe nodded, shrugging.

"So," said Dina, crunching her ice, "why do people find it so easy to believe these rumors?"

"And the answer is?" Gabe sipped his drink, petting Alice, feeling sure whatever Dina came up with would be interesting.

"It's like a bizarre unintentional rescue operation for the powers-that-be. I think it's a Daddy thing. The actual-existing police are bumblers: too much focus on the wrong stuff, too many fuckups, too many threats to our real security and civil liberties. But we need to believe they are all-seeing, all-knowing, all-effective. It's like the mother saying 'Wait till your father gets home,' and then he gets home and all he actually says is 'Listen to your mother.' The system preserves the fiction that Dad is the mighty figure of power, and everybody goes along with it because it makes Dad feel big and important. That's the paradox: we actually give them our power by seeing them as bigger and badder than they really are. It's like we're co-opting ourselves onto their p.r. team. It's like we can't let Daddy be weak."

"The paradoxical rescue," said Gabe, tilting his head to one side, thinking it over.

"Look," said Nick, "whatever you call it, we've got to be realistic. I'm sure somebody's looking for us, but as far as I can tell, they haven't come anywhere close yet. All those rumors on the Net—I guess somebody should tell those people to look past the government's propaganda and their own fears, and amp down the paranoia."

"Aye-aye, commander," said Gabe, jabbing the buttons on his Hawaiian shirt as if they were part of a control panel. "Dialing down."

"You'd think Clarity would have shown them that," said Dina.

"I don't know," Gabe replied. "That sounds like the advanced course. Maybe a double dose."

CHAPTER 9

❀

The High Holy Days, Rosh HaShanah and Yom Kippur, were only a week away. Dina had set aside the next evening for dinner with Nancy and Ronnie for their annual *cheshbon ha-nefesh*—soul inventory—taking stock of where they'd missed the mark in the year gone by and where they wanted to aim in the year ahead. She had something like that old back-to-school feeling: excited anticipation whipped to a froth with a shot of anxiety. When she tuned into the sensations bubbling through her body, it surprised her to notice that positive feelings dominated the mixture.

As Dina walked outside to collect the newspaper, Alice raced right between her feet and out the open door, nearly tripping her. The morning was already heating up, yet the tiniest suggestion of fall could be sensed in the air, a delicate freshness threading through the warmth. Although there hadn't been anything resembling a frost, a few leaves on the liquidambar tree across the street were stained with red. The bronze chrysanthemum was beginning to bloom, sending its bittersweet scent aloft. The cool sidewalk felt wonderful on Dina's soles, rough and smooth at the same time.

These weeks back at work hadn't been as difficult as Dina had anticipated. Only a few strategy sessions had touched so directly on Clarity that she'd needed to watch herself, and the rising tide of questioning and exploration had lifted the governor's boat a little bit too—there'd been more grappling with real issues and a little less of what Gabe called casuistry. Every morning, there had been some agreeable surprise in the paper, some new magic worked by Clarity. The only words Dina could bring to mind for the almost maternal sensations she derived from this news were dusty Yiddish from her girlhood: *nachus*, pride such as a parent feels in a child's accomplishments; *kvell*, brag, what it made her want to do.

Just a few more months, Dina thought, dragging her toes along the sidewalk, *and instead of asphalt and the morning paper, I'll be walking on a hillside, smelling the grass and flowers.*

She stopped dead in her tracks, listening to the echo of her own thoughts. She asked herself if that was really her plan, to move in with Nick. It had slipped out so easily, like an idea waiting—eager—to be born. Yet Dina wasn't aware of having made any such decision. Unwrapping the paper, she rolled the notion around in her mind, noticing that she liked its taste. Idly, she glanced at the headlines.

And immediately wished she hadn't. "Clarity Hoax Unmasked," stared out at her from page one, just below the fold.

> WASHINGTON—After exhaustive testing by a National Institutes of Mental Health team working with the cooperation of commercial nanotechnology enterprises, scientists have concluded that the material known as Clarity contains no active ingredients or mechanisms, including microscopic mechanisms that might interact with the human brain.
>
> Clarity samples were obtained from a variety of sources and tested in the laboratory, including tests on live animal subjects. High-powered microscopes, spectrum chromatography, and post-mortems on lab animals were deployed in an effort to detect Clarity's active properties. Some samples were contaminated with other drugs such as methamphetamine. But as NIMH spokesman Dr. Alvin Buchman said today, in the vast majority of those conforming to the Clarity pattern (small white tablets stamped with the letter C), nothing other than a sugar-based placebo could be detected in the tablets themselves or in the blood or brains of lab animals injected with the material.
>
> An FBI spokesperson who commented on condition of anonymity said it was too soon to make any statement on the possible origins or aims of the hoax, but that a team of encryption specialists had been working on e-mail messages from the group calling itself "Vitamin See" and hoped for a breakthrough soon. In response to questioning, the spokesperson acknowledged that without active ingredients, possession or consumption of Clarity itself could not be grounds for prosecution. But he suggested that fraud charges might conceivably be brought against those who had knowingly circulated false claims via federally protected delivery systems such as interstate phone lines and the U.S. Postal Service.

When Dina got back into the house, the phone was ringing. It was Gabe.

"Déjà vu all over again?" he asked. "Or a disinformation campaign?" This was tiring. This was downright boring.

"You saw the *Times*, right?"

"Right, my Captain. I also checked out what the wild waves were saying."

"Let me guess," said Dina. "The story is a fake, a government conspiracy, etcetera."

"Something like that. And that could be true, no? I mean, I admit it is a little far-fetched to think the American government would deceive the citizenry about something like this. But it's just a remote possibility, y'know what I'm saying?" Gabe knew the possibility was more than remote, but deep down inside, he couldn't be sure.

"Ironically, the fact that no allegation against our government is too far-fetched to be believed was one of my strongest motivations for getting into this mess in the first place," said Dina. "What else?"

"Well, we've got some backspin on the front-spin. Here's a lunatic-right site saying that the devils who made this stuff did it so cleverly it becomes undetectable a short time after it's ingested. Like if it's not there, that proves how terrifying it is. And naturally, some jokes are making the rounds. 'Did you hear about the new drug? It's called Idiocy. One hit makes people too stupid to know whether they're high or not.'"

"Oh, God," moaned Dina. *Please, God*, she was thinking, *please, God make this not be true.* But even in desperation, she didn't really believe in what they called petitionary prayer. She sincerely doubted divine intervention was going to save this situation, but she craved it with all her heart. As she tried to hold back the tears, her mind kept running that desperately yearning soundtrack: *please God, please God, please God....*

"Dina," said Gabe, sounding serious and scared. "That stuff about encryption experts. You said we were safe. Do you think we can be traced?" *You promised me*, he was thinking, feeling eight years old and all dressed up in his Sunday go-to-prison clothes.

"Gary says absolutely no, and Nick trusts him."

"Do *you* trust him?" Gabe kicked himself for having waited this long to ask. He suspected his fear of coming to the attention of law enforcement authorities was a little stronger—and a little better-grounded in reality—than Dina's. Why hadn't he done more to protect himself? What had he been thinking?

Dina ran a short movie in her head. It featured FBI agents seizing her computer, then interrogating her in a conference room at the governor's office—followed by total humiliation as she filed in handcuffs past the entire staff. When Gabe came trailing into the frame behind her, she snapped off the picture. "I've got to go see Nick," she said. "I'm going to call in sick. Delete everything, okay? I mean *everything*."

"Aye-aye."

Dina hung up and dialed the office. With the telephone receiver cradled uncomfortably between her ear and her left shoulder, she opened her word-processing program and began deleting files, using the utility Nick had given her, the one that pulverized them into unrecoverable bits and bytes. There weren't many, just a few press release drafts, but she needed to get rid of the e-mail too, and there was more of that.

At this hour, she assumed the office voicemail would pick up her call, allowing her to leave a quick message, no questions asked, then get back to deleting. But the phone was answered by Elena, startling Dina. "Elena, what are you doing there at seven a.m.?"

"Oh, I had some stuff I couldn't get to yesterday. I like to be the first one here. It's so quiet, you wouldn't believe how much I can get done."

"Well," said Dina, "I'm afraid I'm not going to get anything done today. I must have eaten something bad, because I feel awful."

"Oh, I'm sorry. I'll leave a note at the front desk if anyone calls."

"Okay," said Dina, ready to ring off.

"Dina, wait. Did you see the story about Clarity this morning?"

"I did."

"What do you think?"

Dina sighed. "I don't know, Elena. When you and I talked about this before—remember when that 'Sixty Minutes' story came out?—you said it couldn't be nothing, based on what happened to your boyfriend and his brother."

"That's right," said Elena. "I guess it's a cover-up. But I don't know. There are already all these jokes on the Internet. I've gotten about six e-mails from people in the east, I guess they've been up for hours. Anyway, I suppose we'll know soon enough. Feel better!"

❧   ❧   ❧

Dina drove to Healdsburg more focused on the stuff in her head than on the road. Compulsive repetition of far-fetched scenarios that might magically explain it all alternated with reruns of shocking betrayal and—when she could manage to change the channel—planning her next steps. Maybe she could move to the country, get a job as someone's cook or babysitter; maybe go to a monastery. Reaching the turnoff to Nick's house was like being awakened from a dream. She was amazed she'd made it all this way without getting a speeding ticket or causing a car wreck. When she saw the row of mailboxes that heralded the rutted, winding road to his place, Dina's heart thumped like a sledgehammer. Knocking at Nick's door, she could still see the cloud of dust her car had raised racing up the hill.

Nick answered wearing a wary expression, but it split into an ecstatic grin as soon as he saw it was Dina who'd knocked. "You!" he cried, sweeping her into his arms. "No one ever arrives here unannounced. I thought you were the narcs—old reflex."

"I guess you wouldn't have anything to fear from them though, would you?" she muttered into his shoulder.

Nick pulled back to look at Dina's face. What he saw echoed the rigidity he'd felt in his arms: mouth set in a bitter line, black eyes, a feverish complexion. "Dina, what's wrong? What happened?"

"I guess you haven't been on the computer yet, huh?"

A crooked half-smile lingered on Nick's face, the residue of pleasure. "No. I was just puttering around, getting into the day." Watching Dina's face, he stopped smiling, annoyance beginning to show. He grabbed her shoulders. "Dina! What's wrong?"

Dina pulled away, prying the morning paper out of her bag. She pointed to the Clarity hoax headline. "Don't give me more of that 'Sixty Minutes' bullshit, Nick. They're saying they had the big guns in to look at it and Clarity is zero: no nanobots, no nothing. The Internet is full of jokes about it! Is this what we wanted, Nick? To do something that will make people even more cynical?" She took a deep, sobbing breath. "Gabe says it's a government cover-up. Is it? If not, you have two seconds to tell me why you set me up this way." *Then I have a lifetime to chew over why I let you*, she thought.

Nick's eyes darted from floor to ceiling, as if he could find the answer written on a wall. *Busted*, said his inner voice. *You dunce. You hapless fuckup.* Nick lifted his hands halfway into a shrug. His mouth worked, but nothing came out. *Surprise, asshole*, the voice said. *What did you think would happen?*

Dina felt a pain in her stomach, a cold lump of undigested pain swelling into anger, pressing, pressing hard. Her limbs felt weak, as if someone had suddenly let the air out. Turning on her heels, she tossed the paper onto the couch. "A s-s-souvenir," she stuttered, her voice breaking. "I never want to see you again. Don't call me, don't write me. If you want to know what I'm going to do about this, listen to the news: my press conference will be tomorrow noon on the capitol steps."

❦   ❦   ❦

Dina managed to avoid a traffic citation or an accident on the return trip too, making it home in record time, then marching straight to her workroom to issue a final Vitamin See press release announcing the next day's press conference.

After that, she sat for hours in front of the computer, watching the Gandhi footage over and over again, kicking herself for criminal stupidity. Her stomach felt like a pool of quicksand. When she finally made her self go to the bathroom to relieve her aching bladder, the glimpse she caught in the mirror scared her: she looked like the victim of a mugging, all wild hair, smudged eyes and bruised mouth in a bloodless face.

In between Gandhi reruns, Dina tried to draft her statement to the media, but she could never get through more than a few words without deleting. When her back hurt from sitting too long in one spot, she paced the hallway, crying, picking her way around the shards of glass that used to protect Nick's photo, which now lay on the floor in shreds. Alice paced with her, o-o-w-ling all the way. Feeling exhausted, Dina lay down on the bed and said her bedtime prayer over and over. But sleep was impossible, so she got up again and repeated the cycle.

The phone rang incessantly, but Dina never picked up. Nancy called, still ignorant of Dina's involvement, wanting to gossip about the Clarity story. Gabe phoned to commiserate. Dina knew Nick was up all night too, because every few minutes, she got an instant message or heard the answering machine beep, then his plaintive voice beseeching her to answer the phone. "I know you feel betrayed," said Nick's voice in the distance, muffled like a man in a cave or underwater, "but, please, Dina, I'm begging you. Please hear me out."

At about three a.m. she turned off the telephone ringer and the sound on the phone machine and canceled instant messaging. But the silence didn't help her know what she wanted to say to the media the next day.

She must have fallen asleep eventually, because she awakened at seven having to pee, with a keyboard imprint on her left cheek and a long line of ssssssssssssssss on the computer screen. She splashed water on her face and turned the phone back on. It rang instantly, and acting on reflex, she answered it. It was Gabe.

"Dina, I've been worried about you. Didn't you get my messages?"

"I'm sorry, Gabe. At first I was too depressed to talk, and then I sort of went incommunicado after the forty-seventh message from Nick. Did you get my announcement of the press conference?"

"Yes, I did. I'll be there with bells on—or at least lurking in the back with my collar turned up and my hat brim turned down. What are you going to say, anyway? But wait—first, tell me, what did Nick say? Do the little robots jump out as soon as you swallow the pill, or what?"

"Nick didn't say a goddamn thing. I asked him to his face, and all he gave me was silence. And now I have no idea what *I'm* going to say. What do you think I should say?"

"Well, I know this is radical, Dina, but how about nothing? I mean, that works for me: just because you call a press conference doesn't mean you have to show up. It kind of fits with everything else, if you know what I mean."

Dina groaned. "Afraid I do."

"Seriously, honey. Why do you have to do this? What's the point? Can't we just let it go now, chalk it all up to sad experience? You should see the wild waves, anyway: everybody believes there's a hoax, only it's the government doing the hoaxing. All these people took Clarity and they don't believe it's nothing any more than we do. Right?"

"Gabe, listen to what I'm saying. I confronted Nick with it, and he didn't say a single word. Not one syllable. It's a hoax, all right, and I'm perpetrator number one, and I can't just pretend I'm not and hide my head. I'm a fool and an idiot. I was trying to wake people up from the big trance, and I just put another huge boulder on the tomb of democracy. After this, I predict it will sleep forever." She groaned again.

"Okay, girl scout. Only if there is some kind of prosecution for abusing the Internet or something, and you show up for this press conference, you'll be giving them the defendant—you. Far be it from me to think about myself, but let me just mention that if they know about you, I don't think it's going to be too hard for them to find me. You know what I mean? And I don't want to go to jail."

"Gabe, listen. Clarity was crap, and that's a big shock. That is totally fucked. But they aren't going to be able to send us to jail, and no way am I going to implicate you in anything. They're just blowing smoke. We haven't broken any laws, period. One of the first calls I placed yesterday was to a lawyer for the Electronic Frontier Foundation. We aren't going to be arrested, Gabe. There can't be any charge. There could conceivably be a lawsuit, someone could claim they'd been harmed by the whole Clarity thing and sue me—like some corporation that put a lot of money into nanofilters. But I'm not naming any names, Gabe, even if they put bamboo slivers under my fingernails. And if by some miracle they can break the encryption, they're going to find that just about everything came from my computer."

"Well, y'know, I'm just thinking out loud, but I wonder if 'just about everything' will be enough to satisfy them. Do you want to take that risk?"

"What risk? Between you and me, maybe we could pay the photocopying costs on a lawsuit, which doesn't make us the best targets. Lawsuits are about money, and we have the shallowest pockets in town. Besides, if it did come out—and I'm promising you in blood that no one is going to learn your name from me—you'd become legendary as the viral-marketing expert who launched Clarity. You should be able to take that to the bank."

"The plaintiffs in my lawsuit will be delighted to know that."

"Gabe, the thing is, I can't just flush my conscience because I fucked up. We did this to show people they could see through the cover stories, right? And now I'm going to let the government and the media be the ones who write *this* story? I'm going to let *their* version stand as the truth? If I'm not willing to stand up and take my licks if I have to," she sighed, "what was the point?"

Gabe shrugged, defeated in his attempt to discourage Dina. At least he could tell Lance the story now, stop lying. That was some kind of relief. "Be careful, okay?"

"It's too late to start now," Dina said. "When you go into the office will you say you talked to me and I'm still not well enough to come in?"

"Sure. What's a little off-white lie after all this?"

🍁   🍁   🍁

Dina changed her clothes three times before leaving, choosing the outfit that made Alice o-o-w-l the least, a black pantsuit. For once, she applied her make-up carefully, but all the concealer in the world couldn't make a dent in her despair. She didn't have a statement to hand out to the press because she hadn't managed to cobble one together from the scraps of her self-loathing. She decided to ad lib on four words she'd hand-printed on a file card in her pocket:

apologize, grovel, grovel again

Before locking the door, she felt in her pocket, just to be sure the card was still there. *As if I needed a reminder*, Dina laughed to herself, feeling a tear start to trail through the double coat of blusher she'd applied in a vain attempt to impersonate her former self. When she pulled the key from the lock and turned around, Nick was standing there. Her heart leapt into her mouth, crowding out the bitter residue of her laugh.

"Glad to see you smiling, lady, even if it's not for me. Even if the sight of me chases it away." Nick's hands were jammed in his pants pockets, shoulders hunched like someone trying to keep warm on a cold day, but the temperature was nearly seventy degrees.

"I'm not glad to see anything about you. I told you to stay away." Dina's hands shook so violently, she dropped her keys.

Nick picked them up.

"Dina, I'm so sorry." His red-rimmed eyes filled with tears.

"Why don't you just change your name to Sorry?" she asked him. "Then you could eliminate all the unnecessary steps. Just apologize as soon as you meet someone: 'Hello, I'm Sorry.'"

"Dina, listen to me. You were out the door before I could even get a message from my brain to my speech center." *Very scientific*, said his inner voice. *That should get her.* Nick felt a little explosion in his stomach, like a hot rock dropped into a bowl of water.

"Too many tiny robots blocking the way?" Another infuriating tear escaped, following the first down Dina's cheek. She wiped it away with the back of her hand.

"Very funny. Listen, Dina, this is just as much my mess as yours."

Her skeptical look stopped him in his tracks.

"No," he continued, "it's more, way more my mess than yours. Please, please, please let me do this with you. After that, if you want, I'll disappear. If it's still what you want, I swear on my life I'll never bother you again."

In Dina's mind, a battle raged. *Don't listen to him*, one side said. *You know the snake is lying because his mouth is moving. Remember* t'shuvah, said the other side. *Never too late, never too far to make that turn. Give him a chance to do it.*

"Okay," she said, sniffling, "I'll let you drive me there, but I'm not guaranteeing any more than that. I don't entirely trust myself to make the drive in one piece, anyway. Or maybe that's wishful thinking."

"Perish the thought," said Nick.

"Yeah? Give me one good reason for living."

"I love you."

"So all the lies—the huge fucking lies—those were little gestures of love?"

"No. At first I just did it for the reason I said, to keep something going between us. I didn't think we could make a drug to your specifications, but I figured we could spend a lot of time together trying. Then, after the 'Sixty Minutes' thing, I kept on doing it because, as far as I could see, it was actually working: people were waking up. Not only were we together, but there were little outbreaks of awareness all over the country. The *Wizard of Oz* all over again."

"The *Wizard of Oz*?"

"Yeah, like all the things the characters in that story want—a heart, a brain, courage—what each of them is actually given is only a symbol of their desires, but that makes them smart and brave and loving anyway, because they believe that is what's happening. So I convinced myself I couldn't come out from behind the curtain—not while it was working."

"Yeah, if I ever want to speak to you again," she told Nick, "we can talk about that crock of shit."

Nick opened the door for Dina, but instead of sliding into the seat she remained standing, hugging the open door like a shield. "What about Gary?" she asked. "Was he in on this, or did you make him up too?"

"I did the nanotech research myself. Anybody with a connection to the Internet could have done that. But yeah, he's into the data-encryption thing these days. I told him I needed it for something I wanted to keep real quiet, but it wasn't illegal. I can't see how he could have known it was about Clarity, but I guess he'll find out today."

"Do you think he'll feel used?" Dina asked with a sour smirk.

"I don't think so, but I'm getting the idea I'm not the best judge of that," said Nick, closing the car door.

Once they were underway, Dina pulled out her file card and began despairing anew of turning her pathetic notes into something worth expressing. "If I only had a brain," she said. "I've been thinking all night about what to say and drawing a blank. Everything sounds self-justifying or lame. I keep imagining that the sound bite will be me saying, 'I apologize to the American people,' like some asshole politician who had sex with his intern. The real points of how and why it all happened won't get through any more than they usually do." She blew her nose. "And before you say it, let me stipulate that it's only just and fair. Why should I be treated any differently than anyone else by the media-machine I helped to support?"

"I wasn't going to say it," Nick told her. He glanced at the card. "Apologize, grovel, grovel again," he read. "It has a certain simplicity, but I know what you mean." He handed her two sheets of folded paper. "Since this is my responsibility too, I thought about what needed to be put out here, and I took the liberty of making some notes. Just take a look."

Dina started to unfold the paper as they turned into the long drive up to the capitol steps. But she stopped, alarmed, when Nick muttered, "Oh-oh." The drive was crammed with people: camera crews, still photographers, lots of alert-looking men and women in blazers, clutching notebooks or tape recorders.

"Can we please turn around now?" Dina asked plaintively, her stomach aching. But even if she had been serious, it was too late. Reporters surrounded Nick's car, calling out questions. Then miraculously, they stopped: Dina's face was familiar to the press corps; as soon as they recognized her, they lost interest. All the media knew was that the press conference had been called by the group named Vitamin See. They assumed Dina just happened to blunder onto the scene on her way to work in the governor's office.

"Hey, Dina," said Jeanette Woo. "For a second there, I thought you were the mysterious Vitamin See person. There's supposed to be a press conference here in a few minutes. Have you heard about it?" She craned her neck, hoping to see another car.

Dina took a deep breath and whispered to Nick. "Oh, God! Now what?" Suddenly, she was desperately glad he was there—that she didn't have to face this alone—and just as suddenly, she hated herself for feeling that way.

Nick turned off the ignition and got out of the car, holding up his hands to ward off the crowd.

"It's just Dina Meyer," Jeanette called to her colleagues, who immediately subsided into impatience.

"Maybe this press conference is a hoax too," said a cameraman.

Nick opened Dina's door and helped her out. Arm in arm, they walked to the top of the stairs, no one paying them any mind other than Elena and her cohort standing just inside the glass doors. Elena waved tentatively, then looked confused.

Nick pried the folded paper from Dina's hand and smoothed its wrinkles. "Let's try this," he whispered. "Less temptation to grovel, I promise. I'll cue you."

Dina nodded. *What the hell. I got into this by trusting Nick. Why stop now? Might as well be hanged for a sheep as a goat.*

She whistled, loudly. "Hey," she waved, "I'm up here. Vitamin See, that's me—us, I mean."

As the reporters and crew members turned en masse, mouths open in astonishment, Nick began to read quietly from his paper, one sentence at a time, waiting for Dina to repeat each one before starting the next. "Ladies and gentlemen..." Nick whispered.

It seemed crazy to feel comforted by the sound of Nick's voice in her ear—the voice of her betrayer—to find reassurance in his warm breath, his familiar smell, the pressure of his hand on her elbow. But Dina did. Her shaky voice smoothed out as she went on.

"Ladies and gentlemen," she said, "I'm here today to tell you a hoax story, and to apologize for my part in it. But I also have to say the hoax was on me."

Dina caught sight of Gabe at the back of the crowd, right where he said he'd be. He didn't so much wave as lurch in her direction. Then she saw Nancy leading a group of students toward the crowd, and Ronnie standing by herself, wearing dark glasses and a tight smile. When Dina glanced back at Gabe, his lurch had become a shrug. She guessed he'd called Nancy for reinforcements.

"Half a year ago," Dina continued, "I was in despair at the state of our society, and unable to see any way to change it. To me, it seemed obvious that we have the power to fix everything that is broken in our society, but for some reason, a great many of us can't even conceive of using that power. I wanted to awaken Americans, but I didn't know how.

"Then a crackpot idea came to me: create a new drug, something with no destructive effects, something that could wake people up and enable them to see through the cover stories and falsehoods that we are asked to accept every day. I wanted to awaken people out of the common trance. This was my idea alone, and other than my companion today, Nick Emerson, no one shares responsibility for it."

After this last sentence, Dina caught her breath. To the best of her knowledge, Nick had never made a public declaration of any kind in his life, especially one that could make him the object of uncomfortable attention. He always flew under the radar. Repeating his whispered words of self-disclosure, she felt something knit together. Owning up was Nick's *t'shuvah*. Writing this statement was making his *tikkun*.

Moving a little closer, she allowing her shoulder to press against Nick's chest while the *Shehechiyanu* prayer sped through her mind:

> *Baruch atah Adonai, Eloheynu Melech ha'olam, shehechiyanu,*
> *vekee-imanu, vehig-iyanu, lazman hazeh.*
> Blessed are you, the Force that rules the universe, who has
> kept us in life, made us flourish, and made it possible for us to
> reach this moment.

When Nick whispered the next line of his script, he punctuated it with a kiss on Dina's ear.

"I was persuaded that making a drug to these specifications was possible," she told the crowd. "I was fooled. If we could design drugs like that to order, we'd have one that made you happy regardless of your life situation, and one that kept you young and thin forever. But I really wanted to believe it was possible, so I did. When I issued the Vitamin See bulletins, I truly believed that Clarity was what it purported to be. I was convinced by someone I loved, who loved and wanted to please me, and I am truly sorry for that."

Dina sneaked a glance at Nick. He was staring at her with an intensity that almost burned her skin.

"I took Clarity myself, and found I was able to talk about subjects that had seemed taboo before. Many of my friends reported similar experiences. I've read about them on the Internet and in print publications; I've seen them on television and in public gatherings. Yesterday, I would have said we were in the midst of a societal sea change catalyzed by Clarity. All of you are familiar with some of extraordinary social-action projects, the changes on campus, even the changes in news coverage that we have traced to the spread of Clarity. I daresay some of you have experienced it for yourselves."

There was nervous laughter from the crowd. Nancy made an excited little wave at chest-height. Nick squeezed Dina's elbow and whispered again. She repeated his words.

"If there was nothing in Clarity, why did it work? My guess is that the answer has to do with expectations. We told people to expect to see through lies, to be able to question what they saw and to say what had been unspeakable. I think taking the pill gave many of us permission to do those things, to take a hard look at ourselves and others, to bring our full awareness to what we'd usually done in an automatic or thoughtless way.

"As far as I'm concerned, our little experiment succeeded, because all those things we read about and saw and experienced on Clarity were real: all those people asking questions that pierced the armor of official statements; all those people standing up to petty tyrants; all those people who refused to accept the cover story—they were real. The way the rich and powerful tried to protect themselves from the truth; that was real too.

"So, ladies and gentlemen of the press, here's the sound bite you've been wanting. We can have clarity any day, anytime, with nothing but our own hearts and minds. We can be awake in our lives, rather than letting ourselves be lulled to sleep. Clarity was launched in mid-March. Before you dismiss it, please consider what's happened in less than half a year of people believing they had the power to see and speak truth.

"I want to close by asking every person to do what I plan to do when I go home. Stand in front of the mirror, look myself in the eye and apologize: 'I'm sorry I ever settled for anything less than seeking and speaking truth as I saw it.' After that, what happens next is up to all of us."

Dina gazed at the crowd for a few seconds, letting the roar bubble up around her. Gabe, grinning, blew her a kiss. Nancy talked excitedly with her students. Ronnie was dabbing at her eyes with a handkerchief.

Ignoring a hail of questions, Nick and Dina made their way back to the car, holding hands and grinning from ear to ear. Along their route, reporters talked animatedly into their microphones and cellphones. It was a little like channel-surfing, only live.

Jeanette Woo stood at the foot of the stairs, her back to the capitol dome. Facing a camera, wearing the perky fixed smile of the TV personality, she spoke with animation. Evidently, her segment would close that night's program, because as Dina and Nick let themselves into the car, the words she spoke sounded like a sign-off: "This is Jeanette Woo for KXYZ in Sacramento, and that's the news for September 10th, 2001."

"Where to?" asked Nick, slipping Dina's key into the ignition.

✳   ✳   ✳

0-595-31531-3